The Bu...

by Tim Kelly

Baker's Plays
c/o **Samuel French, Inc.**
45 West 25 Street
New York, NY 10010
bakersplays.com

NOTICE

This book is offered for sale at the price quoted only on the understanding that, if any additional copies of the whole or any part are necessary for its production, such additional copies will be purchased. The attention of all purchasers is directed to the following: this work is fully protected under the copyright laws of the United States of America, the British Commonwealth, including Canada, and all other countries of the Copyright Union. Violations of the Copyright Law are punishable by fine or imprisonment, or both. The copying or duplication of this work or any part of this work, by hand or by any process, is an infringement of the copyright and will be vigorously prosecuted.

This play may not be produced by amateurs or professionals for public or private performance without first submitting application for performing rights. Licensing fees are due on all performances whether for charity or gain, or whether admission is charged or not. Since performance of this play without the payment of the licensing fee renders anybody participating liable to severe penalties imposed by the law, anybody acting in this play should be sure, before doing so, that the licensing fee has been paid. Professional rights, reading rights, radio broadcasting, television and all mechanical rights, etc. are strictly reserved. Application for performing rights should be made directly to BAKER'S PLAYS.

No one shall commit or authorize any act or omission by which the copyright of, or the right to copyright, this play may be impaired. No one shall make any changes in this play for the purpose of production.

Publication of this play does not imply availability for performance. Both amateurs and professionals considering a production are strongly advised in their own interest to apply to Baker's Plays for written permission before starting rehearsals, advertising, or booking a theatre.

Whenever the play is produced, the author's name must be carried in all publicity, advertising and programs. Also, the following notice must appear on all printed programs, "Produced by special arrangement with Baker's Plays."

Licensing fees for THE BUTLER DID IT are based on a per performance rate and payable one week in advance of the production.

Please consult the Baker's Plays website at www.bakersplays.com or our current print catalogue for up to date licensing fee information.

CHARACTERS

(In Order of Appearance)

HAVERSHAM — *A young housemaid, an ex-convict.*
RITA — *A social secretary.*
MISS MAPLE — *A well-known society hostess.*
FATHER WHITE — *A mystery writer.*
CHANDLER MARLOWE — *Another.*
LOUIE FAN — *Another.*
RICK — *Another.*
LAURA — *Another.*
PETER FLIMSEY — *Another.*
CHARITY — *Another.*
MABEL DUPRE — *An adventuress.*
PHARAOH LINK — *A San Francisco police detective.*

STORY OF THE PLAY

Here's a delightful comedy that spoofs English mystery plays, but with a decidedly American flavor. Miss Maple, a society dowager noted for her "imaginative" weekend parties, invites a group of detective writers to eerie Ravenswood Manor on Turkey Island, where they are to assume the personalities of their fictional characters. The hostess has arranged all sorts of amusing "incidents." Everything from the mystery voice on the radio to the menacing face at the window. Secrets abound in the creepy old mansion. Why does the social secretary carry a hatbox everywhere she goes? Who's the corpse in the wine cellar? And how about the astonishing female who arrives via helicopter during a howling storm? When an actual murder takes place, each of the "guests" realizes he or she is marked for death. The outraged hostess offers an immense reward to the "detective" who brings the killer to justice. What an assortment of zany sleuths! An inscrutable Oriental, a seedy gumshoe, a scholarly clergyman, a sophisticated New York couple, an intellectual type who idolizes Sherlock Holmes. When they're not busy tripping over the clues, they trip over each other. The laughs collide with thrills and the climax is a seat-grabber as the true killer is unmasked and almost everyone turns out to be someone else. Can be played as farce or humorous satire. Ideal for all groups.

". . . Successfully interweaves all the classic elements with an imaginative approach . . . a stylish cross between *Ten Little Indians* and *The Cat and the Canary* . . . Great fun and strictly for laughs . . ." Stewart, *Sun Valley* (Ca.) *Green Sheet* . . . "Kelly knows how to write a spiney mystery with a generous injection of wild humor . . ." Jarrett, *Arizona Journal.*

"THE BUTLER DID IT" is a spoof on the classic mystery plays. To be effective the cast must not overdo, or burlesque the subject matter. It should be played perfectly straight in the manner of a serious melodrama, with special attention given to atmosphere and timing. Don't rush it. Naturally, to the audience, much of it will appear absurd and the serious approach hilarious — therein lies much of the fun.

T. K.

"THE BUTLER DID IT"

ACT I

SETTING: *The sitting room of Ravenswood Manor, on Turkey Island, off the coast of San Francisco. It's a shadowy enclave with a brooding quality "made for mystery." DOWN RIGHT there's an exit or servant's door leading to other rooms, including the kitchen. UP CENTER is a small hallway that leads OFFSTAGE for the second story. STAGE LEFT are doors, possibly French doors, that open onto an unseen balcony. Depending on the individual stage size, the set is generous with lamps, bric-a-brac, carpets, furniture. However, the essential pieces are as follows: a fireplace with mantel STAGE RIGHT, with a large portrait hanging above. The subject is a dour, but impressive-looking gentleman. On the mantel there are three figurines. UP RIGHT there is a console. UP LEFT a bookcase. DOWN LEFT there is a desk, chair, and wastebasket. There is a sofa DOWN RIGHT CENTER and a small table and comfortable chair LEFT CENTER. Prior to CURTAIN, SOUND of a MOTORBOAT approaching the island.*

AT RISE: HAVERSHAM, *a maid, is standing at the French doors, one of which is open. She stares off.* **Haversham** *is a mousey creature cursed with a case of the sniffles. Her uniform hangs on her body as if it were two sizes too large. She wears large glasses.*

Haversham. (*Rubbing her arms*) Brrrrrr. Looks like another day for foul weather. There's a storm brewing. I can feel it in my bad toe. (*Calls UPSTAGE*) They're almost here, Miss Maple. The motorboat's at the dock. (**Haversham** *looks OFF again. Sound of MOTORBOAT CUTTING ENGINE.* **Rita Eyelesbarrow** *ENTERS UPSTAGE CENTER carrying a large hatbox*)

Rita. Must you shout, Haversham? No one in this house is deaf that I know of. (*Moves to LEFT CENTER table, puts down the hatbox*)

Haversham. (*Turns*) Oh, it's you, Miss Eyelesbarrow. I thought it was Miss Maple I heard coming down the stairs.

Rita. She'll be along directly. (*Takes lid off the hatbox*) Can you see how many have come over on the motorboat?

Haversham. (*Looks*) Not at this distance. The fog's rolling in. Miss Maple said they'd all come, though.

Rita. (*Perfunctory*) Did she? (*Smiles at hatbox contents*)

Haversham. (*Notices*) New hat?

Rita. (*Quickly puts back the cover*) Never mind about this hatbox.

Haversham. No need to get jangled. I was only asking.

Rita. You tend to your duties, I'll tend to mine.

(**Rita** *EXITS DOWNSTAGE RIGHT with the hatbox.* **Haversham** *makes a face after her*)

Haversham. (*Mimics*) You tend to your duties, I'll tend to mine.

Miss Maple's Voice. Haversham, have my guests arrived?

Haversham. They're at the landing, Miss Maple. (*Looks OFF*) I think they're all here.

(**Miss Maple** *ENTERS UPSTAGE CENTER, a commanding dowager with a lively sense of adventure*)

Miss Maple. Not one of them will fail to show up. I guarantee it. (*She moves to sofa, sits*)

Haversham. You don't even know them.

Miss Maple. That's what will make this weekend such fun. You mustn't say I don't know them. I know them quite well.

Haversham. (*Moves behind LEFT CENTER chair*) Miss Eyelesbarrow said you were all going to be strangers to one another.

Miss Maple. In one sense that is correct. In another sense that is erroneous. (**Haversham** *doesn't understand. Sniffles*) I do wish you wouldn't sniffle. It's distracting.

Haversham. Yes, ma'am.

Miss Maple. And at dinner please don't wipe your nose on your apron.

Haversham. No, ma'am.

Miss Maple. What's the matter with your uniform?

Haversham. How do you mean, Miss Maple?

Miss Maple. Looks large enough for half-a-dozen people. Can't you take it in?

Haversham. Wouldn't do no good. No matter what I put on it'll look like a potato sack.

Miss Maple. If you don't sniffle perhaps no one will notice the uniform.

Haversham. (*Sniffles*) Yes, ma'am.

Miss Maple. Where is Rita?

Rita. (*ENTERS DOWNSTAGE RIGHT*) I'm right here, Miss Maple.

Miss Maple. (*Turns*) You startled me. You do have a habit of creeping up on one.

Haversham. Like poison ivy.

Miss Maple. Haversham, you're forgetting yourself.

Haversham. Sorry, ma'am. (*She sniffles;* **Rita** *bristles*)

Miss Maple. Rita, where is the guest list? I seem to have misplaced it.

Rita. (*CROSSES*) On the desk, Miss Maple.

Miss Maple. The most logical place. No wonder I didn't think of it. (*To* **Haversham**) You're certain you'll be able to handle the kitchen?

Haversham. Won't be no trouble — not when the cook and helper come over from San Francisco.

Rita. (*Picks up some paper*) The agency said we could expect them later this evening. It was the best they could do.

Miss Maple. We'll manage. The list, Rita.

(**Rita** *CROSSES to sofa, hands* **Miss Maple** *the paper*)

Haversham. Beg pardon, Miss Maple. I'm not sure I understood.

(**Miss Maple** *scans the list with the aid of some glasses*)

Miss Maple. Understood what?

Haversham. You said your weekend guests were strangers — yet they weren't.

Miss Maple. (*Laughs good-naturedly*) I mean I know them by their writings.

Rita. (*Superior*) I don't expect Haversham reads a great deal.

Miss Maple. Surely, you've read a mystery or two?

Haversham. Can't say that I have. I like gothic romance, and stories about nurses in love with doctors. Once in a while I enjoy a horror comic. If the cover is gory enough.

Rita. (*Horrified*) Merciful heavens.

Miss Maple. Ladies, ladies, please. I insist on decorum at all times.

Rita. (*Apologetic*) Of course.

Haversham. Whatever you say, ma'am.

Miss Maple. (*Taps the paper*) Each guest is a famous mystery writer. He or she is not coming as himself, or herself as the case may be. He — or she — will arrive as his or her — "creation."

Haversham. Creation?

Miss Maple. Each of these guests will spend the weekend as his or her alter-ego.

Rita. I don't think she understands.

Haversham. (*Sniffles*) I'm trying to.

Miss Maple. They will appear as the detective hero or heroine of their books. They will not use their real names or personalities. They're coming from all over the country. Jolly fun.

Rita. (*Unimpressed*) Yes, ma'am.

Miss Maple. I do suspect they know of my "little project." Few mystery writers don't, despite all the secrecy.

Haversham. Little project?

Miss Maple. It's no concern of yours.

Haversham. No, ma'am.

Miss Maple. Just see that the biscuits are warm and the sherry room temperature.

Haversham. Yes, ma'am.

Miss Maple. (*The list*) Let me see. We have Louie Fan, the famous Oriental detective. Father White — he uses the psychological approach. Peter Flimsey — he's very much in the Sherlock Holmes school.

Haversham. He's a student?

Miss Maple. Haversham, you're quite hopeless.

Haversham. I expect I am. (*She sniffles*)

Miss Maple. Run down to the beach and guide them up.

Haversham. I wish the cook and helper would hurry and get here. (*She EXITS LEFT*)

Rita. Do you really think Haversham is suited to this work?

Miss Maple. I promised the parole people I would give her a home. We must be patient with her.

Rita. (*Surprised*) Parole people. You mean she's an ex-convict?

Miss Maple. I mean she's still a convict.

Rita. Still a convict?

Miss Maple. Rita, stop repeating everything I say. You're sounding like a mynah bird. The truth is simple enough. She's on a work program.

Rita. Work program? (**Miss Maple** *freezes her with a censuring look*) Sorry.

Miss Maple. If she works out well her sentence is reduced and she's put on permanent parole. Much will depend on my report.

Rita. What was her, uh — *crime?*

Miss Maple. I don't recall exactly. Some unpleasantness with a hatchet, I believe.

Rita. (*Moves to doors, stares out*) A hatchet!

Miss Maple. Compose yourself, Rita. There'll be quite enough melodrama when my guests arrive. (*The list*) Chandler Marlowe — now there's a man to reckon with. Seedy, down and out, but intelligent in a brutish sort of way. A true male chauvinist.

Rita. I wish I had known about Haversham before I took this job. She doesn't like me, you know.

Miss Maple. (*Ignores her, concentrates on the list*) And Rick and Laura Carlyle. What a witty couple! So sophisticated, so urbane. I'll enjoy their company.

Rita. (*Wringing her hands in despair*) "Unpleasantness with a hatchet" could mean almost anything. What if the storm is as bad as the one last week? We were cut off for two days.

Miss Maple. We're well-stocked with foodstuffs. No worry.

Rita. (*Alarmed*) Haversham? I recall the name. It was a famous case.

> (*As* **Rita** *becomes more and more uneasy about the "ex-convict and her hatchet,"* **Miss Maple** *becomes more and more delighted with the guest list*)

Miss Maple. I must say I had second thoughts about inviting Charity Haze, bit too much like James Bond for my taste. Still, she's a superb bridge player. (*Puts down the list*) All and all a delightful *menage.*

Haversham's Voice. Come along. She's waiting. Lucky you got across before the storm.

> (*AD LIBS of arrivals from STAGE LEFT*)

Miss Maple. (*Stands*) They've arrived. Excellent.

> (**Rita** *moves to bookcase. First one in is* **Father White.** *He wears a clerical collar, carries a rolled umbrella. His manner is slightly doddering*)

Father White. (*To* **Rita**) Ah, you must be Miss Maple. Delighted, delighted.

Rita. I'm not Miss Maple.

Father White. Eh?

Miss Maple. I am Miss Maple.

> (*They meet STAGE CENTER, shake hands*)

Father White. I'd know you anywhere. Delighted, delighted.

Miss Maple. You must be Father White.

Father White. How did you guess?

Miss Maple. Hardly a guess. (*Indicates*) Your clerical collar.

Father White. Tsk, tsk. First rule of psychological detection: Disregard the obvious. Concentrate on the possible. I might be Louie Fan in disguise.

Miss Maple. (*Enchanted*) Touche. You're a master. (*Nods*) My social secretary and companion, Miss Eylesbarrow.

Father White. How do you do, my dear.

Rita. Welcome to Turkey Island.

Father White. To the best of knowledge only one other island in history has been called Turkey. A battle was fought there. In the Agean Sea. Fourth Century B.C. Spartans versus the Maltese.

Rita. (*Indifferent*) I don't think there's any connection. This island used to be a turkey farm.

Father White. (*Disappointed*) Oh.

Miss Maple. (*Indicates sofa*) Please be seated. Sherry and warm biscuits shortly.

> (*He sits.* **Chandler Marlowe,** *a "tough private eye" type wearing a fedora, raincoat, ENTERS. His hands are in his pockets. His voice is like raw hamburger, talks out of the side of his mouth*)

Miss Maple. (*Playfully*) I wonder who this could be?

Chandler. (*Turns profile*) Take a look at this thin nose, Sister. These gray eyes. This jaw of stone. It ain't Charity Haze.

Miss Maple. No, it ain't. (*Catches herself*) You're a wonder, Mr. Marlowe. Your dialogue is infectious.

Chandler. (*Smug*) I know.

Miss Maple. My social secretary and companion, Miss Eyelesbarrow.

Chandler. (*Tips his hat*) How do, sister.

Rita. Welcome to Turkey Island.

Miss Maple. (*Indicates chair at desk*) Please be seated. Sherry and warm biscuits shortly.

> (*He moves to the desk, stops, makes a distasteful face and silently repeats "Sherry and warm biscuits?"* **Louis Fan** *ENTERS.* **Chandler** *sits on edge of desk*)

Miss Maple. Unmistakably Mr. Fan.

Louie. First rule of Far East detection: Disregard the obvious. I might be Laura Carlyle in drag.

> (*This is not likely. His "accent" is terrible. He, like* **Chandler,** *wears a hat, but it sits on his head sideways. He has a thin pencilled moustache and wispy chin beard. He speaks staccato fashion*)

Miss Maple. My social secretary and companion —

Louie. No need. I overheard on the balcony. Welcome to Turkey Island. (*Moves to painting*) Most unusual portrait.

> (*LAUGHTER from OFF LEFT followed by entrance of the debonair* **Rick** *and* **Laura Carlyle.**
>
> **Rick** *carries a stuffed dog*)

Miss Maple. How good of you to accept my invitation. I'd know you anywhere. Mr. and Mrs. Carlyle.

Chandler. Not necessarily. They could be the cook and helper you're expecting.

Miss Maple. We're going to have such a good time. You've brought your little dog.

Rick. We couldn't take along our real bow-wow.

Laura. Gets sea-sick.

Rick. I said to Laura, who's going to know it's Rick and Laura without their pooch Napoleon.

Louie. (*Takes out small fan, fans himself*) Almost anyone.

Miss Maple. Do make yourselves comfortable. (*She indicates sofa and LEFT CENTER chair*)

Chandler. (*Flat*) Sherry and warm biscuits shortly.

    (**Laura** *sits beside* **Father White** *on sofa,* **Rick** *LEFT CENTER.* **Peter Flimsey** *ENTERS, the very model of a proper English gentleman*)

Miss Maple. Welcome, welcome, Mr. Flimsey. Delighted to have you on Turkey Island.

Peter. I could hardly resist a weekend at any establishment with the name of Ravenswood Manor. It conjures up pictures of the English moors — dark, brooding, mysterious.

Miss Maple. Ooooooh. You talk the way you write. Splendid. My spinal fluid has turned to frost.

    (**Peter** *steps to her, takes her hand, kisses it*)

Rick. (*Appreciatively*) He's a continental gentleman, Laura.

Laura. One of a vanishing breed, Rick.

Chandler. Don't look sanitary to me, slobbering over a dame's knuckles.

Peter. (*Without turning*) I detect the dubious "charm" of Chandler Marlowe.

Chandler. (*Shoves out desk chair*) Park it here, Flimsey.

    (**Peter** *CROSSES, sits*)

Father White. Are we all here?

Miss Maple. I believe so.

Rita. No, Miss Maple. There's one more.

Miss Maple. One more?

Rita. Charity Haze.

Miss Maple. Silly of me. I forgot. (*Faces doors*) Don't keep us waiting, Miss Haze. Come in. (*All face doors*) Come in, Charity.

Chandler. (*Admiringly*) Charity Haze is some woman.

Come on in, baby.

(*Pause.* **Haversham,** *sniffling, ENTERS*)

Haversham. I don't think my sniffles is clearing up, Miss Maple. I think I'm coming down with something.

Miss Maple. Where's Charity Haze?

Haversham. Who?

Rita. The other lady on the boat.

Haversham. What's in this room is it.

Father White. She wasn't with us on the boat. We assumed she arrived earlier.

Miss Maple. (*Pouts*) I've never had an invitation of mine ignored.

Rita. Maybe she'll come on the other boat.

Miss Maple. Unless the storm blows up. Go along, Haversham. Fetch refreshments.

(**Haversham** *CROSSES DOWNSTAGE RIGHT and OUT, sniffling*)

Laura. I wonder who does her dresses?

Miss Maple. I thought we'd just snack until dinner time. I do hope you all like Blue Cheese fondue.

(**Chandler** *makes another sour face and silently repeats "Blue cheese fondue?"*)

Rita. I'll see that everything's prepared upstairs.

Miss Maple. Thank you, Rita.

(**Rita** *EXITS UPSTAGE CENTER*)

Louie. Interesting woman, that Miss Eyelesbarrow. Has she been with you long?

Miss Maple. Barely a month. Why do you ask?

Louie. When the moment is ripe, I shall harvest my deduction.

Father White. There's no need to act so mysterious, Mr. Chan. (*Corrects himself*) I mean Fan.

Chandler. We going to sit around and chew the fat?

Rick. It's either that or Blue Cheese fondue.

Chandler. Let's chew the fat.

Miss Maple. Please, please, dear guests. We mustn't get off the subject. There are ground rules.

Laura. I'm concerned about the storm.

Miss Maple. There's absolutely nothing to worry about.

(*SCREAM from DOWNSTAGE RIGHT.* **Laura** *hugs* **Father White.** **Rick** *stands.* Others *tense*)

Rick. What was that?

Chandler. (*Stands, takes out a revolver*) I'll handle this.

(**Haversham** *comes running back in*)

Haversham. (*Excited*) Miss Maple, Miss Maple, Miss Maple.

Father White. What's wrong with the young woman?

Haversham. Miss Maple, Miss Maple, Miss Maple.

Chandler. She got a problem or is she advertising pancake syrup?

Haversham. (*Frantic*) Miss Maple, Miss Maple, Miss Maple.

Miss Maple. (*A command*) Haversham, get a hold of yourself!

(*Which is precisely what* **Haversham** *does, wrapping her arms tightly around her body*)

Peter. She's hysterical.

Miss Maple. I don't see anything amusing in her condition. Haversham, take a deep breath. (*She does*) Another. (*Repeats*) Good. Now, tell us what happened. Why did you scream like that?

Haversham. It's the only way I know how to scream.

Miss Maple. I mean — what frightened you?

Haversham. I saw a face at the window.

All. Face at the window?

Haversham. A man's face.

Peter. Can you describe him?

Haversham. I don't think so. He had his nose pressed up against the window pane.

Miss Maple. That's what you get for reading comics with gory covers. Probably the man from the boat.

Haversham. No, I'd recognize him.

Father White. Perhaps it was a peeping tom.

Miss Maple. Ravenswood Manor would be unsuitable terrain. No one lives here except myself, Haversham and Rita.

Chandler. (*To* **Father White**) She's got a point.

Miss Maple. Storms always frighten Haversham. (*To* **Haversham**) The refreshments.

Haversham. (*Leery*) Yes, ma'am. (*EXITS DOWNSTAGE RIGHT*)

Rick. Hmmmmm. How long has Haversham worked

for you?

Miss Maple. Not long. Why do you ask?

Rick. I seem to recall the face.

Laura. It's not one you'd forget in a hurry. Especially in that dress.

Miss Maple. (*Claps her hands for attention*) Your attention, please. (**Rick** *and* **Chandler** *sit*) I will go over the ground rules and then we shall proceed with our charade. If you don't know me personally, and none of you do, you know of my reputation for amusing weekend parties. (*Faint applause*) I am recognized as an outstanding hostess with a fine imagination for all that is bizarre and unique.

Peter. The same was said of Sherlock Holmes.

Miss Maple. Then I am in first-rate company. You've all done well so far.

Father White. You couldn't tell us from our literary counterparts?

Miss Maple. No. That's what makes it so charming. However — (**All** *tense*) — I insist that you keep up the "little game" at all times. I forbid you to use your real names. (*Laughs gaily*) I'll be watching . . . and listening. (**All** *smile, relax*) If the weekend turns out the way I trust it will, you will all receive wonderful news. News that will benefit you — *financially*. (**All** *sit up, alert*) I trust you are all willing to play along?

Ad Libs. Yes.

Of course.

Why not?

Sounds like fun.

Wonderful idea.

Chandler. I'm with you, Sister. All the way.

Miss Maple. (*Girlish laughter*) Chandler, you're a rare customer.

Chandler. I like to think of myself as well-done.

> (**Miss Maple** *laughs. The others laugh to humor her. She EXITS DOWNSTAGE RIGHT. The instant she's off, the laughter ceases abruptly*)

Rick. What's her game?

Peter. You cannot be serious?

Laura. Rick is always serious when he hears the word "financially."

Louie. Money, like sweet-smelling flowers, attracts the bumblebees.
Chandler. You calling us bumblebees?
Louie. If shoe fits.
Chandler. Bumblebees don't wear shoes.
Father White. A figure of speech, Chandler. Dreadful syntax, but colorful. Typical of the amusing Louie Fan.
(**Louie** *bows, fans*)
Laura. May I ask something?
Chandler. Be my guest, Sister.
Laura. Why are we all talking like this? Miss Maple is out of the room.
Peter. How do you mean?
Laura. We can relax. Be ourselves. Talk normally.
(**Others** *stare at her. She looks from one to the other*)
Chandler. I am talking normally. This is the way I always talk.
Peter. Quite.
Father White. I wear this collar, but my speech is my own.
Louie. Man who loses identity seldom finds himself.
Peter. Whatever that means.
Rick. Laura and me aren't any different here than we are at home in our fashionable East Side Manhattan apartment. (*Shakes stuffed dog*) Right, Napoleon? (*He fakes a dog's bark*)
Peter. (*Stands, moves to bookcase*) Miss Maple is a most enterprising woman. She's also, as the vulgarism goes — "filthy rich." If she wants another scalp on her "famous parties" list, I'll volunteer mine. I'll enjoy humoring her.
Louie. Most generous.
Chandler. Who you kidding, Flimsey? (*He stands, moves CENTER.* **Peter** *studies some book*) Sure, the old Maple dame is famous for her weekend parties, but the way I hear it, she's going to open up a chain of bookstores.
All. Bookstores?
Chandler. Detective bookstores.
All. Detective bookstores!
Chandler. (*Sly*) 'Course, none of you knew about that,

did you? (*All look about, innocent, avoiding his glance*)
We're all here for the same reason and it ain't to sample
Blue Cheese fondue.
Father White. Forget the fondue.
Chandler. That won't be easy.
Rick. In other words, you believe we're all here to win
Miss Maple's favor.
Peter. Thus insuring our detective novels a place on
the shelves, as it were.
Chandler. That's the name of the game.
Laura. Well, what of it? I don't imagine the Charity
Haze books are going to be on Miss Maple's shelves.
Business is business and if Miss Maple wants to play
games before placing an order with the publishers, I say
— why not?
Peter. Bravo.
Father White. (*To* **Laura**) I imagine you're glad about
this. Most of your stuff is out of print.
Laura. (*Stands, indignant*) If you weren't a man of the
cloth, I'd have a few choice words for you. (*She moves
UPSTAGE, stands by hallway*)
Chandler. Fan's novels aren't doing much better. Even
the Nostalgia Book Club turned him down.
Louie. (*Fanning furiously*) Beware of the dragon's
wrath.
Chandler. The only thing dragging about you is your
book sales.
        (**Chandler** *moves back to the desk, sits.* **Louie**
        fans wildly)
Rick. This is no way to start the weekend. This should
be a light and happy occasion. How about some music?
Laura. Good idea. I'll get something. (*Moves to console*) I hope the static won't be too heavy. The storm
could cause interference. (*She snaps some dial. The
RADIO BLARES immediately — loud and clear*)
Radio. We interrupt this program of light chamber
music to bring you a special bulletin. A dangerous murderer has escaped from the Marin County Institute for
the Criminally Insane. Known only as "The Killer of
Forty Faces," the prisoner seized a rowboat at dawn and
was last seen heading into a fog bank on the approach
to Turkey Island. Now, back to our Mozart concerto.

Laura. (*SNAPS OFF the RADIO*) Can it be true?
Louie. What about the mysterious face the maid saw at the window?
Peter. Forty faces? There's a master of disguise!
Miss Maple. (*ENTERS DOWNSTAGE RIGHT*) Sherry and biscuits.

      (**Haversham** *follows in with a tray of glasses and biscuits, which she sets down on some table*)
Father White. My congratulations, Miss Maple.
Miss Maple. What are you talking about?
Father White. The classic touch, I've used it several times in my own novels.
Rick. Isolated house on a lonely island and — then — a radio or television flash. *Mad Killer on the prowl!*
Miss Maple. (*Disappointed*) You're too clever for me. But I did think it was amusing.
All. (*AD-LIBBING*) A masterstroke! Wonderful! (*They applaud*)
Miss Maple. Too kind, too kind. It's`not easy to fool detective writers. Haversham, serve the sherry.
Haversham. (*Sniffles*) Yes, ma'am.
Rick. Let's hear it again.
Father White. By all means. It was most amusing.

      (*The writers are anxious to please* **Miss Maple** *and are overdoing their eagerness*)
Chandler. Couldn't've done better myself.
Peter. Witty, that's what it was, Miss Maple.
Laura. Here goes. (*She snaps on RADIO again. Only this time, the MALE VOICE is different. Deep, eerie, ominous*)
Radio. I accuse!
Miss Maple. Oh, dear, that's not it.
Radio. I accuse!
Chandler. Get it like you had it the last time.
Laura. (*Snapping dial back and forth*) It's all there is.
Radio. Step back from the console!
Laura. (*Jumps back*) Oh!
Miss Maple. (*Disturbed*) I don't understand.
Radio. Chandler Marlowe —
Chandler. Me?
Radio. Chandler Marlowe, I accuse you of a foul crime. You cannot escape your past.

Laura. Foul crime?

Chandler. (*Uneasy*) It's a gag, that's all. (*To* **Miss Maple**) Right, Sister?

Radio. Louie Fan — remember that night in Shanghai? I accuse you of treachery.

Louie. (*Tenses, fans himself nervously*) Have never visited illustrious city of Shanghai.

Radio. Rick and Laura Carlyle — what does the name "tulip" mean to you both? (*They react*) I accuse you of unforgivable deceit.

Laura. (*Wary*) Tulip, tulip?

Rick. I think I recognize that voice.

Radio. Father White — why are you really here at Ravenswood Manor?

Father White. (*Flustered*) I — I — I was invited.

Radio. I accuse you of sinsiter motives and shaming your calling.

Peter. It would seem you've all been up to some mischief.

Radio. Peter Flimsey — what actually happened on the cricket field at Eton?

Peter. (*Flabbergasted*) Eton? I haven't been there in years.

Radio. I accuse you of dishonor.
> (*With each "accusation," the tension in the room increases*)

Haversham. Shall I set out the biscuits?

Miss Maple. Hold your tongue.
> (*Which is what* **Haversham** *does, sticking out her tongue and holding it with her thumb and finger*)

Miss Maple. Are you trying to be funny?

Haversham. Sorry. It's my nerves.

Radio. Charity Haze — I accuse you of murder.

Haversham. (*Rattled*) Murder? I don't know anything about murder. (*All look to* **Haversham**) What are you looking at me for? I'm not Charity Haze.

Radio. You have heard the accusations, You cannot escape. You will be punished.

Chandler. (*Trying to control his uneasiness*) It's a gag, I tell you.

Radio. Miss Maple?

Miss Maple. (*Without thinking*) Yes?

Radio. What is the real secret of Ravenswood Manor?
(Pause)
Haversham. Is that all?
Radio. That is all.
(SOUND of STATIC)
Laura. *(Turning dial)* I can't get anything. It's all static.
    (**Laura** *snaps it OFF. Everyone is on edge, looking to one another in the hope someone will speak first*)
Rick. Uh, uh — you've outdone yourself, Miss Maple.
Laura. Very, uh — "original." *(Weakly)* Ha, ha.
Father White. *(Applauds weakly)* Effective, theatrical, once again — classic. I, myself, used the technique in my best-seller *Crime at Coffin Corner.*
Peter. I used it in *Murder at the Masquerade.*
Louie. Respectful submit my title, serialized in several popular magazines — *Crime is a Puzzlement.*
Chandler. Don't forget I used the gimmick in *Murder Mops Up.*
Rick. Laura and I employed the accusing-record ploy in our clever and sophisticated — *Manhattan Murders.*
Laura. *(On edge)* I think I'd like to go to my room now.
Rick. Sounds sensible. Could do with a slap of after-shave.
Chandler. Point the way, Sister.
Miss Maple. Are you speaking to me? *(Thinks)* Oh, of course, you are. I forgot our little charade for the moment. *(Points)* Through the hallway, up the stairs. You'll find your name on your door.
    (*The "guests" move into the hallway and out.* **Louie** *remains*)
Louie. Most delightful interlude, honorable hostess.
Miss Maple. Thank you, Mr. Moto.
Louie. Fan.
Miss Maple. Fan?
Haversham. His name is Mr. Fan, Miss Maple.
Miss Maple. Yes, yes, of course.
Louie. May present a question?
Miss Maple. Please do.
Louie. *(He points to painting)* Man in portrait. Honorable ancestor?
Miss Maple. Yes, yes, my father.

Louie. His name, please?

Miss Maple. His name? Uh — Mr. Maple.

Louie. Most compelling face your father. Please to be excused. (*He bows, EXITS*)

Haversham. What about these biscuits? They'll get stale.

Miss Maple. (*Frantic*) Who put that last tape on the machine? (*She moves to it*)

Haversham. I thought you did.

Miss Maple. Don't be foolish. My tape was the first tape.

Haversham. They was scared — your guests.

Miss Maple. You noticed that, too?

Haversham. They tried to cover up, but I know a roomful of scared pigeons when I see them.

(*THUNDER, the ROOM LIGHTS FLICKER*)

Miss Maple. We're in for a bad time with the storm, I'm afraid.

Haversham. The lights might go.

Miss Maple. Why isn't Rita here when I need her?

Rita. (*ENTERS UPSTAGE CENTER with the hat box*) I'm right here, Miss Maple.

Miss Maple. Rita, why didn't you tell me about this tape?

Rita. The one you put on the machine?

Miss Maple. No, no — the one accusing my guests of dark crimes.

Rita. I don't know a thing about it, Miss Maple.

Miss Maple. Why do you so often carry that hat box? What's in the hat box, Rita?

Rita. (*Hugs it protectively*) Nothing.

Miss Maple. Then why carry it?

Rita. I'd better check on the supplies the motorboat unloaded on the dock. (*CROSSES to balcony doors, EXITS*)

Miss Maple. She's acting strangely.

Haversham. A weird customer, Miss Maple. She put on the other tape, I bet. I'd keep an eye on her if I was you.

Miss Maple. Well, you're not me. Come along. To the kitchen. I want to check on the fondue.

(**Miss Maple** *EXITS DOWNSTAGE RIGHT,* **Haversham** *follows. Another ROAR of THUN-*

DER, followed by a DIMMING UP AND DOWN of the LIGHTS. **Rick** *ENTERS from hallway; he's alone)*

Rick. Someone say something about biscuits and sherry? Anyone about?

(**Rick** *CROSSES to the tray, takes a glass and a biscuit, moves CENTER. MORE THUNDER.* **Rita** *returns, still clutching the hat box)*

Rita. I didn't know you were downstairs, Mr. Carlyle. I thought you were with the others.

Rick. Came down a moment ago. You been outside?

Rita. I was going to the dock, but it's starting to rain heavily, and the wind is up.

Rick. What's in the hat box?

Rita. *(As if the question is driving her insane)* What would you expect to find in a hat box!? *(She hurries across stage.* **Rick** *stares after her, bewildered. She turns, assumes a civil tone, smiles)* Sir. *(She EXITS)*

Rick. *(To himself)* Hmmm. Strange lady. *(Sits, sips his sherry, puts down glass. Suddenly, he gives a cry — as if something were stuck in his throat. He leaps up, clutching his throat, making terrible sounds for several seconds)* I've been poisoned! I'm dying, dying. *(Gagging, he drops to his knees)* Dying, dying — (Collapses) — Dead. *(Dies in an exaggerated fashion. On cue, the* **"guests"** *rush in from hallway, AD-LIBBING alarm)*

Ad-Libs. What was that cry?
Who cried out?
What's happening?
Sounded like Rick Carlyle.
Etc.

(**Peter** *and* **Father White** *move LEFT.* **Louie, Laura** *move RIGHT.* **Chandler** *stands UPSTAGE CENTER. They do not see the body)*

Laura. It did sound like Rick.

Peter. What do you supoose he was yelling about?

Father White. Sounded as if he were in pain.

Chandler. Maybe he got into the fondue.

(**Louie** *is at the tray with the glasses of sherry and plate of biscuits)*

Louie. Most curious.

Laura. What is?

Louie. One biscuit missing, one glass with sherry gone.

Peter. What of it?

    (**Miss Maple, Haversham, Rita,** *with the hat box, ENTER DOWNSTAGE RIGHT*)

Miss Maple. We heard a scream.

Rita. All the way to the kitchen.

Louie. Perhaps you could enlighten us, Miss Maple.

Miss Maple. About what?

Louie. Missing glass with sherry and absent biscuit.

Haversham. (*The corpse*) Who's he?

Laura. Louie Fan, a well-known Oriental detective.

Haversham. Not him. (*Points to corpse*) Him.

    (*All look*)

Chandler. It's Rick.

Laura. It can't be!

Father White. Don't look, Mrs. Carlyle.

Laura. Whatever you think best.

    (**Laura** *turns her back.* **Chandler** *moves to the corpse, kneels down beside him, investigates*)

Peter. Is he — dead?

Chandler. (*Confirms*) Dead.

Father White. How dead?

Chandler. How dead can you get?

Peter. (*Wary*) The voice on the radio. It said we'd be punished.

    (*THUNDER. A figurine falls from the mantle.* **Haversham** *screams*)

Laura. Now what?

Haversham. A figurine fell off the mantle.

    (**Father White** *moves to the figurine, picks it up. It's broken in two*)

Father White. Broken.

Louie. I think I understand. Most classic. As each of us is "punished," a figurine will fall from the mantle. Nine in this room, nine figurines on the mantle.

Rita. Three.

Louie. Explain, please.

Rita. There aren't nine figurines on the mantle, there are only three.

Louie. (*Surprised*) Only three? (*Frowns*) Must readjust deduction.

Chandler. Never mind about that. This is serious. We've got a dead man here.

Miss Maple. This isn't turning out as I planned. Chandler, what does it all mean?

Chandler. Mean? It means murder, Miss Maple.

All. (*Aghast*) Murder?

Chandler. Murder on Turkey Island.

 (*All stare at the corpse. THUNDER. LIGHTS FADE, leaving the weekend party in near-silhouette*)

CURTAIN

END OF ACT ONE

ACT II

Scene 1

AT RISE: *Later. The STORM HOWLS outside Ravenswood Manor. Here and there, a LAMP GLOWS in the empty room. An outline of Rick's body has been drawn on the floor. Several moments pass and then, slowly — the bookcase swings open. A flashlight beam is seen and* **Father White** *cautiously ENTERS, guardedly closes the entrance to the "secret passageway."*

Chandler's Voice. (*FROM OUTSIDE*) Hey, Flimsey! Flimsey!

(*Fast,* **Father White** *moves to the sofa, sits, putting the flashlight behind him.* **Chandler,** *his coat wet, ENTERS*)

Father White. Chandler, this is no time to be walking about outside. You'll catch something.

Chandler. Only thing I want to catch is the killer.

Father White. You're quite sure the poor fellow is dead?

Chandler. The killer?

Father White. I mean Rick.

Chandler. Flimsey and me stretched him out on a table down in the wine cellar. He's still there. The dead don't walk.

Father White. Tsk, tsk. I fear Miss Maple's little "charade" has taken a nasty turn.

Chandler. Never saw a murder that wasn't nasty. Nasty murders are my business.

Father White. You're used to crime in the streets.

Chandler. The streets are my beat. Fancy dumps like Ravenswood Manor are a bit rich for my blood.

Laura. (*ENTERS UPSTAGE CENTER*) Am I intruding?

Father White. No, no, my dear. (*Starts to get up*) Do join us.

Laura. Don't get up. (*She moves DOWNSTAGE*)

Chandler. Did you get any sleep, baby?

Laura. Dropped off the minute my head hit the pillow.

Chandler. Grief does that.

27

Laura. (*Notices the damp coat*) Chandler, you're all wet.

Chandler. The dock's almost gone. The storm's torn up the piling. If the cook and helper get here, my name ain't Chandler Marlowe.

Father White. Your name isn't Chandler Marlowe. I mean — really.

Chandler. You're a stickler for details, padre.

Laura. I suppose you're wondering why I've taken Rick's demise so lightly.

Chandler. You ain't exactly used up a box of Kleenex with the waterworks.

Laura. (*A dramatic confession*) Truth of the matter is Rick and I have been estranged for some time. Would you like to hear about it?

Father White. Not really, Laura, my dear. Domestic troubles are quite beyond my comprehension. Man of the cloth and all that.

Chandler. Personal things should be kept personal. I ought to know, I've looked through enough keyholes.

Laura. If you insist. (*Ignoring their replies, she goes into a dramatic confession*) He was interested in another woman.

Father White. Tsk, tsk.

Laura. Or, perhaps, more correctly, another woman was interested in him.

Chandler. Dames will get you every time.

Father White. Do you know the creature?

Laura. Rick or the other woman?

Father White. The other woman.

Laura. In a way. I had a private investigator investigate her.

Father White. What sort of a person was she?

Laura. Fascinating, I suppose, but unscrupulous. Her name was — Mabel Dupre.

Chandler. What is it now?

Laura. What are you talking about?

Chandler. You said her name *was* Mabel Dupre. What does she call herself now?

Laura. (*Annoyed*) That's a stupid question, Chandler.

Chandler. Let's hear a stupid answer.

Laura. A leopard doesn't change its spots. I imagine

her name is still Mabel Dupre.

Chandler. What did the private investigator come up with?

Laura. Almost nothing. She moves around. Never stays long in one place. He did find out one thing of interest.

Father White. Oh?

Laura. She had a violent temper.

Chandler. Sounds like my kind of woman.

Father White. I can well understand the attraction. Mabel Dupre, the flame, Rick Carlyle, the moth.

Chandler. Only he got burned — bad.

Father White. Classic tragedy.

Laura. I loved that man of mine. He'd be by my side today if it weren't for that vampire.

Father White. Speaking of vampires, Miss Maple's library has a fine collection of Victorian novels. Some are quite ghoulish.

Chandler. Not my type of stuff. I cover the pavement.

Father White. Do you think she might be mixed up in your husband's death?

Laura. Miss Maple?

Father White. Miss Dupre.

Laura. A woman like that is capable of anything.

Chandler. You're positive you never crossed paths?

Laura. Never set eyes on her. However, I did hear her voice.

Chandler. When?

Father White. Where?

Laura. In my contemporary Manhattan apartment. Weeks ago. Before the invitation arrived. The phone rang. I answered. The operator said "Person-to-person call from Mabel Dupre for Rick Carlyle." Then I heard her voice.

Chandler. What did she say?

Laura. She said — "Hello."

Father White. What did you say?

Laura. I said — "If you know what's good for you, you'll never try to contact my husband again — or else."

Chandler. Or else what?

Laura. I'd rather not say.

(**Miss Maple** *ENTERS from DOWNSTAGE RIGHT*)

Miss Maple. This is all so distressing. Fun and games are one thing. Murder is quite another.
Chandler. Amen, Sister. Murder ain't no parlor game.
Miss Maple. Chandler, you're all wet.
     (**Laura** *sits LEFT CENTER*)
Chandler. I've been outside.
Miss Maple. Obviously. What am I going to do?
Father White. No telephone anywhere in the house?
Miss Maple. None. No wireless or citizen's band, either.
Chandler. It's a cinch no boat is going to get here until morning.
Miss Maple. What about poor Rick?
Chandler. He ain't going nowhere.
     (**Flimsey** *ENTERS UPSTAGE CENTER*)
Chandler. I thought you were going to give me a hand outside. For all we know, the killer is out there prowling around, waiting for another target.
Miss Maple. You mean he may strike again?
Chandler. (*Straight at* **Laura**) He or — *she*. The female is the deadly species.
     (**Laura** *stiffens*)
Peter. Chandler, you're all —
Chandler. Don't say it, don't say it, or I'll give you a knuckle sandwich.
Laura. Your sort would resort to brute force.
Chandler. It's been the secret of my success.
     (**Louie** *ENTERS DOWNSTAGE RIGHT*)
Louie. If brute force were all, tiger would not fear scorpion.
Chandler. There you go talking about bugs again.
Miss Maple. Mr. Moto, have you discovered anything that might shed light on this terrible affair at Ravenswood Manor?
Father White. Fan.
Miss Maple. What?
Laura. His name is Fan. You said Moto.
Miss Maple. Did I? How peculiar.
Louie. (*Turns DOWNSTAGE RIGHT*) Please to enter.
     (**Rita,** *with hat box, followed by* **Haversham,**
     ENTERS DOWNSTAGE RIGHT)
Miss Maple. You *have* discovered something.
Louie. Please be seated, Miss Maple. Will presently

name murderer of once semifamous Rick Carlyle.

(**Miss Maple** *sits on sofa*)

Ad Libs. What?

Who?

Incredible!

But how —

Etc.

(**Chandler** *moves to desk, sits.* **Peter** *CROSSES DOWN behind LEFT CENTER table.* **Louie** *takes STAGE CENTER*)

Louie. Patience. All will be revealed.

Laura. I have a strong feeling, Mr. Wong, that the murderer's name will begin with the letter "M."

Chandler. Fan.

Laura. What?

Haversham. His name is Fan. You called him Wong.

Laura. I didn't say he was wrong, I said the murderer's name would begin with the letter "M."

Father White. Not wrong — Wong!

Miss Maple. This is getting us nowhere. (*To* **Father White**) I do hope the suspense will last.

Chandler. The guy we need here is Paraoh Link.

All. Who?

Chandler. Top police detective on the Frisco force.

Miss Maple. I'm not unfamiliar with his name. However, since he doesn't write detective fiction, he wasn't on my list of invitees.

Peter. What's all this business about the letter "M?"

Chandler. The deceased was mixed up with another doll.

Father White. Mabel Dupre.

Louie. Please. Know nothing of letter "M."

Haversham. Comes right after "L." (*All give her withering looks*) Sorry.

Miss Maple. Why should this Dupre woman poison Mr. Carlyle?

Laura. I know her sort. Unpredictable, quick-tempered, dangerous. A woman like that will stop at nothing.

Chandler. What's her motive?

Laura. Obvious. Rick preferred me and told her so. Mabel Dupre vowed vengeance.

Peter. Proof?

Laura. No proof. Woman's intuition.

Chandler. Intuition ain't no substitute for logic.

Louie. Must get choo-choo back on track. The clue is in the recording. Killer knew each of us — intimately.

Father White. If you mean the accusations, I have no idea what the fellow was talking about. I am here only because I was invited.

Louie. Killer hates detective mystery writers. Shall now name murderer. (*THUNDER. He points his finger at each person in the room. As he does, they react*) You — you — you — you — you —you — — you are *murderer!* (*With that he points directly at the portrait over the mantel*)

Laura. Miss Maple's father?

Louie. Correction, please. That is portrait of famed historian Ludwig Flush.

Father White. But why should Ludwig Flush want to do us harm?

Louie. Early in his career, Ludwig Flush publish detective novels under pen name of Antonia Cheddar. Failed miserably, turned psychotic, and devoted life to subject of ancient history.

Rita. You mean his sense of frustration is so fierce he'd *punish* successful detective writers?

Chandler. I've heard of weirder customers.

Laura. Where is he now?

Louie. In house.

Ad-Libs. What?
You mean now?
At Ravenswood?
Etc.

Haversham. I know! He must have been the face at the window.

Father White. Could be.

Louie. Not possible.

Miss Maple. Why not?

Louie. Ludwig Flush confined to wheelchair due to advancing age.

Miss Maple. A nice theory, but it won't hold water.

Chandler. Like this coat I'm wearing. It's damper than a lunch counter rag.

Louie. Have proof. (*WALKS OFF DOWNSTAGE RIGHT*)

Laura. What kind of proof, I wonder.
Peter. I'm afraid Mr. Wong gets carried away. He does that in his writings, too. Never could make any sense out of his nonsense. One finds more clarity in a fortune cookie.
Louie. (*RETURNS pushing a wheelchair*) Behold, incriminating evidence.
Father White. A wheelchair? I don't see what that proves.
Louie. Miss Maple, why did you lie? Why you say man in portrait was dishonorable father?
Miss Maple. I had no idea it would come to this.
Laura. You mean — Ludwig Flush is your father?
Miss Maple. I don't mean anything of the sort. I don't know any deranged person by the name of Ludwig Flush.
Louie. But portrait —
Miss Maple. If you must know, there's a hole in that fireplace wall. The portrait fit perfectly, so I used it for covering.
Peter. Where did you get the portrait?
Miss Maple. Where do I get all my interesting pieces? At a garage sale.
All. Garage sale?
Miss Maple. Your entire line of reasoning is absurd.
Louie. But wheelchair —
Haversham. (*Moves behind it, points*) Maybe this'll help. What's written here.
Chandler. What's it say, kid?
Haversham. (*Reads*) "Property of United States Coast Guard."
Father White. Coast Guard?
Haversham. "If found please contact nearest Federal Lighthouse Station."
Laura. If it doesn't belong to Ludwig Flush, how did it get here?
Miss Maple. All sorts of flotsam and jetsam washes up on the beach. It's kept in the cellar, but obviously Mr. Fan felt the wheelchair should be taken upstairs to aid his ridiculous theory.
Louie. (*Fans, moves to bookcase*) Must reconstruct deductions. Most unique case.
Miss Maple. Haversham, get that out of here.
Haversham. Yes, ma'am. (*She wheels OFF the chair*)

Rita. (*Confidentially*) I'm afraid one of the upstairs windows will blow open. Damage could be done to the expensive Oriental.

Chandler. (*Overhears*) Expensive? You can pick up a Louie Fan paperback for two bits.

Rita. I meant the Oriental *carpet*. It's rare.

Chandler. So are you, baby.

Miss Maple. Go along, go along, and take your hat box with you. You're always leaving it about.

Rita. Yes, Miss Maple. (*EXITS UP CENTER*)

Father White. (*Stands, moves to wherever the tray of sherry and bisquits has been set out*) I trust we all realize we could have been wiped out.

Miss Maple. You mean if we ate the bisquits?

Laura. The poison was in the bisquits?

Chandler. I'll give you three to one on the sherry. That stuff will kill you even when it ain't been poisoned.

Father White. Do we fully grasp the seriousness of the situation?

Laura. Cut off from the mainland —

Miss Maple. The storm —

Peter. No communication —

Chandler. A face at the window walking around —

Father White. I think it would be wise if none of us ate or drank anything until morning.

Miss Maple. Until morning?

Father. Until the storm ebbs and we can signal a passing boat.

Louie. If still — alive.

(*THUNDER. All react to Louie's dire words*)

Peter. The poison was not in the sherry or the pastry.

Laura. We all saw the half-empty glass and half-bitten bisquit.

Peter. Stand up, if you would, Mrs. Carlyle.

(*She does.* **Peter** *takes out a magnifying glass*)

Miss Maple. (*Appreciative*) A touch of the master himself. Sherlock Holmes.

Peter. Magnifying glasses have become quite sophisticated since the days of London fog and hansom cabs. This one, for example, magnifies twenty times. It can also identify odors.

Miss Maple. Amazing.

Peter. (*Moves in front of the chair*) One should never be taken in by appearances. It's a capital mistake to theorize before one has all the evidence.

Chandler. So?

Peter. If you'll all look here, you'll see what I mean.

   (*All move to the chair.* **Peter** *points to a spot in the upholstery*)

Peter. There's the spot. (**Laura** *takes the glass, studies the chair*) See it?

Laura. Why, it looks like a little needle.

Peter. Correct.

Chandler. Give me a look. (*He takes the glass, looks. Each person has a turn*)

Peter. Rick Carlyle was murdered by a poisoned *dart*.

All. *Dart?*

Peter. (*Moves toward painting*) I discovered the dart about an hour ago. Since the dart entered the body at an almost straight angle, I surmised it came from the painting. Or, rather, as Miss Maple has explained, the hole in the wall.

   (**Chandler** *crosses to the portrait, studies it*)

Chandler. You're right. One eyeball is missing.

Father White. We're up against a clever killer.

Laura. Either clever, or — mad. How do we know some lunatic didn't get wind of this weekend party, and decided to have a murderous lark?

Miss Maple. You're allowing your imagination to run away with you, my dear.

Laura. Am I? (*Points*) Do you realize I was sitting in that chair?

Miss Maple. Good heavens, you might have been scratched!

Chandler. Mind explaining yourself out of that one, Flimsey?

Peter. I removed the vicious little dart, analyzed the poison, and returned the miniature weapon for the purpose of recreating the murder method. Without the poison it's harmless.

Chandler. I'll give you credit, Flimsey. You're no man's fool.

Peter. I appreciate that, Chandler.

Chandler. I still think we ought to case the island.

Peter. I'm ready.

Chandler. Let's go.

>(**Chandler** *crosses to the doors.* **Peter** *removes the dart*)

Miss Maple. I'm terrified. What man could have done such a thing?

Peter. Aren't you forgetting something, Miss Maple?

Miss Maple. What?

Peter. Poison is a woman's weapon.

Chandler. Come on, before he gets away.

>(**Chandler** *EXITS into the storm.* **Peter** *FOLLOWS*)

Miss Maple. I should see to matters in the kitchen, but I'm frightened of every shadow.

Louie. Would allow my humble protection?

Miss Maple. Thank you, Dan. I appreciate that. (*EXITS DOWNSTAGE RIGHT*)

Louie. (*Follows*) The name is Fan . . . (*Sighs*) Oh, what's the use. (*He EXITS*)

Father White. I think it would be a wise idea if we stayed together.

Laura. You mean — safety in numbers?

Father White. Precisely.

Laura. I don't see how that will protect us from flying darts coated in poison.

Father White. Still, we must admit the killer is a villain of imagination. No pistol shots for this chap.

Laura. Then you're convinced the killer is a male?

Father White. A rogue male, perhaps. Time will tell.

Laura. If your theory is correct then you could be the killer.

Father White. My dear, dear child. You're distraught.

Laura. Or Peter Flimsey, or Chandler Marlowe. Or Louie.

Father White. (*Trying to calm her*) Laura, Laura, calm yourself.

Laura. Stay away from me!

>(*She turns and hurries OUT DOWN RIGHT. SOUND OF STORM. The LIGHTS FLICKER UP AND DOWN.* **Father White** *checks the doors to ascertain that he's alone, moves to bookshelves, pulls them aside so he can enter the secret passage-*

way. **Laura** *SNEAKS BACK IN, STANDS DOWN-STAGE RIGHT, observing. When* **Father White** *IS GONE and the bookshelf back in position,* **Laura** *moves to it, runs her hands over the shelves)*

Laura. There must be a button or lever somewhere.

(**Rita** *ENTERS UP CENTER with the hat box)*

Rita. *(Looks around)* I thought I heard you talking to someone, Mrs. Carlyle.

Laura. *(MOVES DOWN LEFT)* I do that when I'm nervous.

Rita. Would you like a sedative? You must be exhausted. *(Puts down hat box)*

Laura. Sleep is the last thing I want. At least when I'm awake I know I'm alive.

Rita. Poor Miss Maple. She was so counting on a fun weekend.

Laura. It's a raging success. If you have a macabre sense of humor.

Rita. I want to confide in someone.

Laura. What about?

Rita. Haversham. She's on parole. Imprisoned because of some unpleasantness with a hatchet.

Laura. *(Thinks)* Haversham? Hatchet? Of course! I recall the case.

Rita. Be on guard.

Laura. I appreciate your telling me.

(**Rita** *turns, starts to exit DOWN RIGHT)*

Laura. Rita.

(**Rita** *turns)*

Laura. Don't forget your hat box.

(*Quickly,* **Rita** *hurries to the hat box and snatches it up in her arms. SOUND OF HELICOPTER overhead)*

Rita. *(Looks up)* What's that?

(**Miss Maple** *and* **Louie** *ENTER from DOWN RIGHT)*

Miss Maple. There's a helicopter overhead.

Laura. Helicopter?

Miss Maple. Undoubtedly a police helicopter. We're saved. Saved!

(**Chandler** *and* **Peter** *APPEAR at the doors)*

Chandler. You ought to get a look at this.

Peter. It's over the house. You can see the lights through the rain and fog.

(**Louie, Miss Maple, Rita, Laura** *join the men at the door, look OFF STAGE*)

Miss Maple. Is it the police?

Chandler. Don't know, but they put a ladder down. I saw it swinging in the glow.

Laura. Ladder? You mean they're dropping someone down in this weather?

Rita. That would be insane.

Louie. Who would be foolhardy enough to descend to house of murder?

Charity. Charity Haze, that's who.

(*All turn to see* **Charity** *standing DOWN RIGHT, an incredibly capable and attractive young woman in a form-fitting raincoat, helmet and goggles*)

Chandler. Charity, baby, you remember me. Chandler Marlowe. We met at Mardi Gras in New Orleans. I'd know you anywhere.

Charity. Charity Haze isn't your ordinary face in the crowd. (*She removes goggles and helmet*)

Miss Maple. I don't understand. A helicopter?

Charity. I missed the boat. This might be ungracious of me, but I could do with a hot bath.

Rita. I'll prepare one. (*EXITS UP CENTER*)

Miss Maple. I'm your hostess, my dear. (*Introductions*) And this is Mr. Peter Flimsey, and this is Mr. Louie Fan, and —

Charity. Could we hold the introductions 'til after I've had my bath?

Miss Maple. Whatever you say, Charity. Come along, I'll show you to your room. How delightful that you've arrived. You live up to your reputation.

(*They MOVE UP CENTER*)

Charity. Don't suppose I could get a glass of sherry and a bisquit?

(*They're OUT*)

Chandler. (*Admiringly*) What a girl. A package of dynamite.

Louie. Remarkable young woman.

Peter. Exceptional. (*Looks at* **Laura** *who is wide-eyed*) What's the matter with you, Laura?

Laura. (*Points after Charity*) That voice — that voice — I'd know it anywhere! (*Pause*) *Mabel Dupre!*

CURTAIN

END OF SCENE 1

ACT II

Scene 2

AT RISE: *Later. An OCCASIONAL GUSH OF WIND is HEARD.*

Miss Maple *sits on the sofa.* **Chandler** *stands DOWN CENTER.*

Miss Maple. You say you knew Charity from the past?

Chandler. Met her down in Louisiana.

Miss Maple. Louisiana? How romantic.

Chandler. Actually it was kind of muggy. Got mildew on my gumshoes.

Miss Maple. I must say I'm *terribly* disappointed in Louie. All that business about Ludwig Flush and the wheelchair. Lucky for him the hero of his books isn't so dense.

Chandler. Never read much of him. Too soft for me. I like my crime hard-boiled.

Miss Maple. Murder is not an egg, Chandler.

Chandler. Bad eggs stink and so does murder. There's been a murder in this house. It stinks.

Miss Maple. I had Rita throw an embroidered bedsheet over poor Mr. Carlyle. I thought it was the least I could do.

Chandler. You're a gracious doll.

Miss Maple. I can be gracious and I can be resolute.

(*Charity ENTERS UP CENTER*)

Charity. I feel like a human being, thanks to that hot tub.

(*Chandler gives a long, low whistle*)

Chandler. You look like a human being, baby. My kind of human being.

(**Charity** *moves to DOWN RIGHT end of sofa*)
Miss Maple. Chandler tells me you two met in Louisiana.
Charity. At Mardi Gras.
Miss Maple. How romantic.
Charity. I didn't think so. The weather was muggy and I got mildew on my platforms.
Chandler. Gotta admire any girl who can arrive at a weekend house party during the height of a storm. In a helicopter.
Charity. Don't call me a girl, Chandler. I'm all woman.
Chandler. You can say that again.
Charity. You heard me the first time.
Miss Maple. I was annoyed when you didn't arrive on the boat, then I was relieved.
Charity. Relieved?
Miss Maple. I mean now that we're all apparent targets for some deranged killer.
Charity. You mean Rick Carlyle.
Miss Maple. He's not the killer. He's the victim.
Charity. What's anybody doing about it?
Chandler. We're doing what we can. We're not eating anything. We're not drinking anything.
Miss Maple. Mr. Fan made some preposterous deductions that did nothing but cloud the issue. The man is a buffoon.
Charity. Everyone seems to be taking the murder calmly.
(**Father White** *ENTERS DOWNSTAGE RIGHT*)
Father White. I'm not taking it calmly. I've been down in the wine cellar.
Chandler. What of it?
Father White. There's a body down there.
Miss Maple. Naturally, there's a body down there.
Charity. Or unnaturally.
Miss Maple. Rick Carlyle.
Father White. *He's dead!*
Chandler. He won't get any deader.
Father White. You don't understand. He's *really* dead.
Chandler. You been sampling any of the wares down in that cellar?
Father White. (*Distraught*) I thought it was part of

the game, all part of the charade. I expected him to show up later and tell us it was all a joke.

Miss Maple. Murder is never a joke.

Chandler. Didn't you hear what Flimsey said? A poisoned dart.

Father White. Murder!

Charity. Sit down, Father White. You're weak in your kneecaps.

Father White. I am distraught. Fun and games are one thing —

Chandler. Yeah, yeah. We know. Murder's something else.

(**Father White** *crosses, sits in LEFT CENTER chair*)

Miss Maple. I like realism as well as fantasy in my charades, but I trust you don't believe I'd go as far as murder.

Father White. (*Buries his face in his hands*) I don't know what to believe anymore.

(**Peter** *ENTERS from outside*)

Peter. Can't see a thing. Fog's like black ink.

Father White. Oh, oh, oh. Murder.

Peter. What's the matter with him?

Charity. It's just got to him that the corpse in the wine cellar is a corpse.

Peter. Would you mind explaining that?

Father White. (*Rocking back and forth*) Oh, oh, oh. Murder. Real murder.

Chandler. That's the worst kind. Incurable.

Peter. Looks as if you're gathering for a counsel of war.

Miss Maple. I've asked the others to join me. I do wish they'd get here.

(**Louie** *ENTERS UP CENTER*)

Louie. When honorable hostess requests, honorable guest complies.

Miss Maple. (*Her patience exhausted*) Do shut up.

(**Louie** *fans angrily*)

Chandler. I'll tell you something else, Louie. I don't believe Oriental people talk the way you do.

(**Louie** *fans furiously, steps in front of bookcase*)

Miss Maple. (*Looks around*) Where is Laura? Why isn't she here?

Chandler. She had a bit of a shock.
Miss Maple. Shock?
Charity. Someone murdered her husband.
Chandler. She took that standing up. I don't mean her husband.
Peter. He means you, Miss Haze.
Charity. What have I got to do with Laura Carlyle? I don't know the lady. Read some of her books. Not my brand at all.
Chandler. You're more like me, baby. Ear to the city's asphalt.
Charity. Leave my ear out of it.
    (**Laura** *ENTERS UP CENTER, cold, determined*)
Miss Maple. Ah, there you are. Come and join us.
Laura. I'll sit over here. (*She sits in some chair where she can watch* **Charity**)
Miss Maple. As you wish.
Chandler. (*Moves to desk, sits*) You got something on your mind, Miss Maple?
Miss Maple. I told you, Chandler, I can be gracious, and I can be resolute.
Chandler. Let's hear the resolute.
Miss Maple. Quite. (*She stands*) Ladies and gentlemen, I must aplolgize for the strange turn of events at Ravenswood Manor.
Peter. It's not your fault.
Miss Maple. The point I wish to emphasize *exactly*. I don't want anyone to believe I would stoop so low as to engineer this "misfortune."
Laura. Why would we even think such a thing?
Charity. You mean we might suspect you were out to publicize your new chain of bookstores?
    (*Guests look innocently around the room.* **Charity** *has let the cat out*)
Miss Maple. (*Flat*) What bookstores?
Charity. It's no secret, is it? (*To the others*) Isn't that why we're all here — to make sure our books are on the shelves?
Louie. I am here as tranquil weekend guest, nothing more.
Charity. Nonsense.
Peter. You go right to the heart of the matter, Charity.
Charity. I don't see any reason to pussyfoot.

Miss Maple. So you all knew what I was planning?

Peter. What if we did know? No harm done, is there?

Father White. Why not ask Rick.

Peter. Rick who?

Father White. *The dead man in the cellar!*

Miss Maple. As Mr. Fan would say — "Must get choo-choo back on track." My reputation as a hostess has been impeccable.

Charity. Until now.

Miss Maple. (*Sighs*) Alas. We have no choice but to remain on the island until morning. Is that correct, or isn't it?

Peter. Correct.

Chandler. (*Confirms*) We're stuck here until daylight.

Miss Maple. I will not have my party ruined by an unknown killer whose motive or motives, as yet, are unrevealed.

Charity. Huh?

Miss Maple. I will not bow down to any sinister force. Nothing will change. The charade will continue!

(*Impressed by her fervor, they politely applaud*)

Miss Maple. Forgive me, I didn't mean to get carried away.

Peter. Why continue?

Miss Maple. I want the killer found so he can be punished. Murder is one thing, but the ruination of a weekend party at Ravenswood Manor is quite another.

(*More applause*)

Father White. That's well and good, Miss Maple, but we're detective writers, not the police.

Miss Maple. The police would only bungle the case. Besides, Mr. Flimsey has already shown remarkable talent in deduction.

Chandler. I've been prowling around, on the scent.

Father White. You have a great deal of faith in us.

Miss Maple. Poo. I've already explained my theory. Detective story writers often create sleuths like themselves.

Charity. Only more so.

Miss Maple. Exactly. I've invited you here because you're the best in your field. Prove it. Find the gate-crasher. Let his apprehension be a warning to all other social bores.

Charity. I wouldn't call a murderer a "social bore."

Miss Maple. Who else but a bore would do such a thing?

Chandler. If all else fails we could at least get a pretty good yarn out of this.

Miss Maple. Yarn?

Chandler. A book. I got a title already — *Murder Walks the Fog.*

Louie. *Island of Evil.*

Father White. *Mystery in San Francisco Bay.*

Charity. *The Corpse in the Wine Cellar.*

Laura. *Mad Weekend.*

Miss Maple. The sooner the beast is caught, the sooner we can hand the fellow over to the police with a minimum of publicity.

Louie. Publicity like door, Works both ways.

Miss Maple. Then we're agreed. We will not bow down to the intruder. The charade continues.

Peter. As you wish.

Miss Maple. However —

All. Yes?

Miss Maple. To assure you that I'm not frivolous in my desire to catch this monster, I will award an honorarium to the one who smokes him out.

Charity. How much?

Miss Maple. $25,000!

All. $25,000!

Miss Maple. (*Moves UP CENTER, turns*) You have until sunrise. (*She EXITS*)

Charity. (*Sits on sofa*) I think she means it.

Chandler. She means it.

Peter. She won't stand for anyone disrupting her weekend house party.

Charity. If I find out who did it I won't be adverse to publicity.

Laura. (*Leaps to her feet in a fury*) No, your kind never is!

Charity. My kind?

Laura. Why are we standing here talking? (*Points*) There's the killer! She's the one! *Mabel Dupre!*

Charity. (*Stands*) Mabel who?

Chandler. Easy, baby. That's not the Dupre dame. It's Charity Haze. Take my word for it.

Laura. (*Advancing on* **Charity**) Don't let that phony wig fool you. It's Mabel, I tell you.

Charity. Mabel? Mabel?

Father White. You're making a mistake.

Laura. Take off that wig! (*With that she grabs* **Charity** *by the hair*)

Charity. Ow, ow, ow!!!

Laura. You homewrecker!

Charity. You're crazy!

Laura. Give me that wig!

Charity. Ow, ow, ow!

    (**Laura** *continues to pull at* **Charity,** *who protests loudly. Others move around trying to stop the fracas*)

Fathr White. Laura, control yourself!

Chandler. Let me handle this.

Louie. Most unfortunate.

Peter. Do something, Chandler!

Laura. Give me that wig!

Charity. It's not a wig!

    (**Charity** *winds up and socks* **Laura** *on the chin. She falls back into the LEFT CENTER chair*)

Charity. It's my own hair, you idiot.

Laura. (*Calms down, rubs her cheek*) Thanks, Charity. I needed that.

    (*At this point positions are as follows:* **Laura** *in the chair,* **Charity** *in front of the sofa.* **Chandler** *and* **Peter** *STAGE LEFT,* **Louie** *and* **Father White** *behind the sofa*)

Charity. What was that all about?

Peter. You'll have to forgive her. She's not herself.

Louie. She mistook you for arch rival. Infamous Mabel Dupre.

Chandler. You still pack a mean wallop, Sugar.

Charity. (*Blows on her knuckles*) I can take care of myself, Chandler.

Peter. I think we're making a great mistake.

Father White. In what way?

Peter. I think the clue is in the recording.

Laura. If it is, there's a woman behind it. I feel it.

Chandler. There you go with that woman's intuition again.

Peter. In other words, Laura, you mean — *Cherchez la femme!*
Chandler. Huh?
Father White. Find the woman.
Chandler. What woman?
Peter. It was that famous detective Monsieur Jackal in Dumas' *The Mohicans of Paris* who first used the phrase.
Louie. Who?
Peter. Wearing his green spectacles and constantly dipping into his snuffbox.
Chandler. Huh?
Peter. Forever saying — *Cherchez la femme!*
Laura. Then you agree with me.
Peter. Surely, you all know that Monsieur Jackal was the literary ancestor of all the great ferrets from Victor Hugo's Javert —
Charity. Victor who?
Peter. — to Doyle's Holmes, and years before Hawkshaw.
Chandler. What's a ferret?
Father White. I don't know any Hawkshaw. What's he talking about?
Peter. Your education in the history of detectives is sadly lacking.
Louie. Interesting you use word "history." Suggests name of gentleman in portrait. Ludwig Flush.
Charity. I understand the recording accused me of murder.
Chandler. Yeah.
Charity. Easily explained.
Laura. How?
Charity. Since I've never actually murdered anyone, anyone real, that is, the recording had to mean a popular character in one of my books.
Chandler. I remember. You had a character by the name of Jumbo, a great gumshoe.
Charity. I got bored with him and knocked him off. In print. There was a public outcry. Critics said I "murdered" Jumbo.
Peter. In much the same manner, Doyle caused a sensation when he killed off Sherlock Holmes.

Laura. Interesting, but it's not getting us anywhere.
Louie. Am not sure I can agree. Most interesting explanation. Suggests other possibilities.
> (**Rita** *ENTERS DOWN RIGHT. There's an afghan over her arm*)

Rita. It's getting chilly. I thought someone might need an afghan. I'll put them in the bedrooms, too. (*Puts the afghan over the sofa back*)
Laura. We won't be doing much sleeping.
Rita. Gets quite chilly on the island. (*She EXITS UP CENTER*)
Father White. First time I've seen her without the hat box.
Louie. Curious you should mention hat box. Recalls case of Headless Horseman.
Chandler. I remember that one. A Jockey was murdered by his girlfriend during the Kentucky Derby.
Charity. Why did they call him the Headless Horseman?
> (*Pregnant pause as the terrible implication registers*)

Laura. You mean —
Father White. You mean —
Charity. You mean —
Louie. Miss Eyelesbarrow looks amazingly like missing girlfriend, a female addicted to hats. Noticed similarity as soon as I entered Ravenswood Manor.
Laura. I not worried about the missing girlfriend. I worried about the missing —
Father White. Don't say it, my dear. It's too dreadful to contemplate.
Laura. She could be the lunatic killer!
Chandler. (*Matter-of-fact*) We've got more important things to worry about. I think we should lay out a plan of action.
Father White. What do you suggest?
Chandler. Charity and me will tackle the wine cellar. Louie, you and Father White go over the upstairs with a fine-tooth comb.
Louie. Do not possess such an article. Hee, hee, hee. A small joke.
Chandler. If it was a big joke it wouldn't be any funnier.

Laura. What about me?
Peter. I'll take Laura with me. We'll check around outside.
Laura. Is that wise?
Peter. We'd better stick in pairs.
Laura. I mean going outside. The storm.
Chandler. Just keep thinking about that twenty-five grand.
Laura. (*To* **Peter**) Let's go outside.
Father White. Come along, Louie. (*EXITS UP CEN-TER*)
Louie. You lead, I follow.
Peter. Stay close. (*EXITS out the door,* **Laura** *follows, turns*)
Laura. I am sorry about the wig.
Charity. So's my scalp.
     (**Laura** *smiles, apologetic, EXITS.* **Chandler** *crosses to* **Charity**)
Chandler. Charity, baby, here we are together again.
Charity. Keep your mind on your work, Chandler. Ravenswood Manor isn't Mardi Gras.
Chandler. How about a little kiss for old times' sake?
Charity. (*All business*) Which way is the wine cellar?
Chandler. (*Points DOWN RIGHT*) Down that way. (*He closes his eyes.* **Charity** *EXITS*) Come on, Charity. I'm all puckered up. Give us a kiss. (*He opens his arms for an embrace.* **Chandler** *smacks his lips a few times*) Come on, Sugar. I'm waiting.
     (**Haversham** *ENTERS DOWN RIGHT*)
Chandler. A big hug and kiss for old times' sake. (**Haversham** *sniffles, shrugs. Kisses* **Chandler**) You call that a kiss?
Haversham. I ain't no lover girl.
Chandler. (*Opens his eyes*) You!
Haversham. Who'd you expect?
Chandler. (*Disgusted*) Where's Charity?
Haversham. Down the hall. If she's going to the wine cellar she won't get in.
Chandler. Why not?
Haversham. I locked it.
Chandler. (*Grabs her by the arm*) You can unlock it.
Haversham. The key's by the door!

(**Chandler** *pushes her OFF STAGE. The LIGHTS FLICKER, GUSH OF WIND whips up. The door to the secret passageway opens slightly*)

Miss Maple's Voice. Haversham, Haversham!

(**Miss Maple** *ENTERS UP CENTER*)

Miss Maple. Hello? Anybody about? (*She steps into the room, notices the flickering lights*) Oh, dear. (*Suddenly she senses something is not quite right in the room, starts to turn as the bookcase closes shut. She reacts to the SOUND*) What was that? (*She steps to the bookcase, selects a book*) I'll read. That'll quiet my nerves. (*She moves to the LEFT CENTER chair, sits, reads aloud*) The Case of the Curious Caretaker . . . "I shall never forget the night I arrived at Skull Island . . . no one was there to greet me with the exception of Miss Midwinter the housekeeper, a woman of stern countenance and iron will . . . and I was terrified . . . Perhaps if the boatman had not been blind and mute some of my fears might have been lessened, but, alas, that was not to be . . . Why was the bell in the abandoned tower ringing, I wondered? Did it foretell some dreaded happening . . ." (*As she reads a* **Figure** *in gloves, long coat, hat, face covered by a scarf and dark glasses, ENTERS from secret passageway*) ". . . it wasn't the warmest of welcomes for a governess of sixteen . . . what would I encounter here, in this strange house of ancient rocks and dark emotions . . ." (*She realizes she's not alone, tenses. SOUNDS OF RAIN*) Who's there? (*Panic seizes her*) Who's there, I say? (*She stands, faces the* **Intruder** *who darts back into the passageway and closes the bookcase*) Who are you? No, wait! (*CRASH OF THUNDER. SHOTS RING OUT FROM DOWN RIGHT.* **Miss Maple** *collapses in the chair with a dying groan. SOUND OF RAIN INCREASES*)

Laura's Voice. Hurry!

Peter's Voice. I'm right behind you!

(*They ENTER*)

Laura. Another moment and we'd be drenched.

Peter. If our killer's outside he's a fool as well as a madman.

(**Laura** *tiptoes to* **Miss Maple**)

Laura. Sssssssh.

Peter. Hmmmmmmmm?
Laura. How sweet. She's fallen asleep, like an innocent child.
Peter. Should we wake her?
Laura. Let her sleep. She needs all the rest she can get. (*Gets the afghan and tucks it around* **Miss Maple**) She'll be fine.

(**Laura** *motions that he shouldn't make a sound, and the TWO of them tiptoe OFF UP CENTER.*

The LIGHTS DIM leaving **Miss Maple** *in a cold blue circle. Another figurine falls from the mantel.* **Miss Maple** *SLUMPS. SOUND OF RAIN UP)*

CURTAIN

END OF ACT II

ACT III

AT RISE: *Early morning.* **Miss Maple** *remains slumped over.* **Charity** *and* **Chandler** *ENTER DOWN RIGHT.*

Charity. People murder for one of three reasons, Chandler.

Chandler. I'm listening.

Charity. Profit, revenge . . .

Chandler. What's the third reason?

Charity. I forget, but it will come to me.

(**Louie** *and* **Father White** *ENTER UP CENTER*)

Father White. We've searched everywhere. Not a sign of an intruder.

Charity. Maybe the others have found something outside.

Louie. Not so. They remain upstairs.

Chandler. They were supposed to remain outside.

Father White. The rain forced them in.

Louie. What did you two discover?

(**Chandler** *and* **Charity** *are standing DOWN RIGHT,* **Louie** *and* **Father White** *UP CENTER. They ignore the HOSTESS*)

Charity. There's an embroidered bedsheet over the dead man.

Louie. Perhaps killer in gesture of contrition placed embroidered bedsheet over deceased.

Father White. An embroidered bedsheet does sound a bit extravagant. After all, a plain bedsheet would have done as well.

Louie. Suggest we consider motive behind placing of the embroidered bedsheet over cooling body of Rick Carlyle. Possibly will lead to killer's identity.

Chandler. You guys belong in a museum. The old doll had Rita toss the linen over the victim. Park it, Sugar.

(**Charity** *sits on the sofa.* **Chandler,** *too.* **Father White** *moves to doors, looks out*)

Louie. One less clue to consider.

Chandler. Louie, I don't think you could find yourself in the dark.

51

(Haversham *ENTERS DOWN RIGHT*)

Haversham. It ain't raining so much as before. (*She sniffles*)

Chandler. (*To* **Charity**) Gotta watch that Haversham. She sneaks up when you ain't looking and steals a kiss.

Haversham. (*Defensive*) I don't steal. (*Thinks*) I mean I don't steal no more. I'm reforming.

Father White. What are you talking about?

Haversham. (*Sees* **Miss Maple**) Hello. What's the matter with her?

Father White. Who?

Haversham. (*Nods*) Miss Maple.

(*All look*)

Father White. Bless me, I didn't see her sitting there.

Charity. She's awful still.

Laura. (*ENTERS UP CENTER, overhearing*) Please don't wake her. She's exhausted.

Father White. Is it any wonder?

Chandler. Where's Flimsey?

Laura. Washing his hands.

Father White. "Out, damned spot! Out, I say!"

Haversham. Huh?

Father White. Shakespeare. *Macbeth.* Act Five, scene one. Lady Macbeth attempts to wash away the blood of guilt.

Haversham. Huh?

Louie. Why would man wash hands when he has just entered house from storm?

Haversham. Maybe they were dirty. She don't look right to me.

Charity. Who?

Haversham. Who we been talking about? Miss Maple.

(*All look at the slumped-over figure*)

Laura. Napping, I tell you.

Father White. Should we wake her?

Chandler. Old people need sleep. Let her be.

(**Peter** *ENTERS UP CENTER,* **Laura** *moves to bookcase*)

Peter. Any luck?

Chandler. Naw.

Father White. We've discovered exactly nothing.

Haversham. (*Picks up broken figurine*) It's another one.
Laura. Another what?
Haversham. Another figurine fell off the mantel. It's broken like the first one.
Louie. Most unusual.
Chandler. Anybody got any ideas?
Peter. About what?
Chandler. About anything.
Charity. Why don't we get up a rubber of bridge?
Ad Libs. Splendid.
Why not?
Might relieve tension.
I'll be dummy.
Etc.
> (*Enraged,* **Miss Maple** *flings aside the afghan, and stands*)
Miss Maple. *Outrageous!*
> (*All are startled*)
Miss Maple. Didn't anyone of you realize I was murdered!
Laura. We thought you were asleep.
Miss Maple. Shots rang out. I was slumped over. A figurine fell from the mantel.
Charity. What's going on here?
Miss Maple. I'll tell you what's going on. You're a bunch of incompetents. I arranged for Haversham to fire some blanks to test your reactions and, alas, you've all failed miserably. Ladies and gentlemen, you disappoint me profoundly.
Charity. You were carrying on with the charade, right?
Miss Maple. That, Charity, is self-evident. Since everything else has proven slightly absurd, I'm beginning to doubt that the gentleman in the cellar is truly deceased.
Charity. He's deceased.
Chandler. Take our word for it.
Miss Maple. I shall see for myself. Get the key, Haversham.
Haversham. Yes, ma'am. (*She EXITS*)
> (**Miss Maple** *crosses DOWN RIGHT, turns, denounces her guests with* —)

Miss Maple. *Idiots!* (*She EXITS*)

Laura. (*Calmly*) She's annoyed.

Peter. (Moves DOWN CENTER) I hope this doesn't mean she'll give up the idea of the bookstores.

Charity. We better think up something to calm her down.

(**Rita** *ENTERS UP CENTER with hat box*)

Rita. You must be famished. There's some food that's sealed in its container. We might eat that. No one could tamper with it.

Laura. I am hungry.

Rita. I'll see to it at once. (*Moves DOWNSTAGE RIGHT*)

Louie. One moment.

(**Rita** *turns*)

Rita. What is it, Mr. Tan?

Louie. (*Trying to control his temper*) The name is Fan, not Tan. Louie Fan. (*Holds up fan, speaks as if he were instructing a backward student*) This is a fan. Think of fan. (*Waves it back and forth*) Cools one on a hot day. *Fan.* Understand?

Rita. (*Indignant*) I'm not a child. (*Coolly*) You had something to say to me?

Louie. Must be obvious to all that killer is one of us.

Ad Libs. What?

You can't be serious?

How can you say that?

Louie. Will explain.

Laura. Do.

Louie. Why would sweetheart of heartless jockey take job at Ravenswood Manor?

Chandler. Are you talking about the "Horseman" murder? At the Kentucky Derby?

Louie. I am.

Chandler. He wasn't heartless. He was headless.

Louie. Believe Miss Eyelesbarrow is jockey's sweetheart.

Rita. That's ridiculous.

Louie. Suggest Rita Eyelesbarrow was also sweetheart of Rick Carlyle, and when he wished to end friendship, was struck down as was unfortunate jockey.

Laura. You mean —

Louie. (*Points*) There is murderer.
Laura. You mean —
Louie. Fascinating and unscrupulous —
Laura. You mean —
Louie. Mabel Dupre!
    (*All stare at* **Rita.** *She looks over her shoulder*)
Rita. What's everyone staring at?
Louie. You are Mabel Dupre. You murdered Rick Carlyle.
Laura. I don't want another mistake.
    (**Louie** *takes newspaper clipping from pocket, hands it to* **Laura,** *who moves DOWNSTAGE*)
Louie. Here is photograph from newspaper of unhappy jockey and his mad sweetheart.
Rita. Rubbish.
    (**Chandler** *moves to* **Laura.** *As do* **Father White** *and* **Peter**)
Louie. Note positive resemblance.
    (*All look at clipping and then at* **Rita**)
Louie. Case is solved.
Peter. Uh, Louie.
Louie. Yes?
Peter. The female in this picture is a black woman. Miss Eyelesbarrow is not a black woman.
Charity. (*To* **Louie**) What a meatball. No wonder your books are going out of print.
Louie. Let me see picture. (*He moves to others, takes clipping, studies it*) Hmmmmm. (*To* **Rita**) You are not mad sweetheart.
Rita. Maybe I'm not sweetheart, but I'm certainly mad. Furious! You fool!
    (**Louie** *moves behind others for protection*)
Louie. Unless hat box belongs to jockey's killer.
Charity. Why are we here talking about the Kentucky Derby when Miss Maple is angry with the lot of us? Rita, forgive this — what did you call him?
Rita. I called Mr. Fan a fool.
Charity. Forgive the fool. Please fetch Miss Maple from the wine cellar.
Rita. (*To* **Louie**) You ought to be locked up. You're a menace. (*She EXITS*)

Chandler. (*Moves behind* **Charity**) I gotta hand it to you, Louie. You're one in a million.

Father White. You do get carried away. Two wrong deductions in one evening is quite enough.

Louie. (*Regally*) When all the hens cluck, who can hear the rooster?

> (**Louie** *walks UP RIGHT, stands by console.* **Laura** *moves to LEFT CENTER chair, sits*)

Chandler. I agree with Louie on one point.

Father White. What's that, Chandler?

Chandler. The killer is one of us.

Peter. Why was Rick the only one to get it?

Chandler. (*Vague*) Get what?

Peter. The dart in that chair. (**Laura** *gets up quickly, moves to the doors*) Oh, I am sorry, Laura. That was tactless. No fear, though. I put a piece of metal plate behind the portrait. The passageway the deadly dart took has been sealed.

Chandler. I wish you'd stop talking like one of the characters in your lousy books.

Laura. If only the dawn would get here.

Chandler. Give it time.

> (**Miss Maple** *ENTERS*)

Miss Maple. He's dead. Quite dead. There can be no mistake.

> (**Rita** *ENTERS after* **Miss Maple,** *who moves to sofa and sits*)

Rita. I think I might be able to shed some light on this grisly affair.

Charity. Pitch in.

Rita. Haversham.

Charity. What about her?

Miss Maple. Rita, what I told you was in confidence.

Rita. I don't think we have any right to keep it a secret any longer.

Laura. You mean about Haversham's police record?

Miss Maple. How did you know?

Rita. I told Mrs. Carlyle.

Miss Maple. Haversham isn't homicidal.

Rita. What about the "unpleasantness with the hatchet"?

Louie. Hatchet? Aha, we are back to the hat box.

Miss Maple. Nothing of the sort.

Peter. Haversham? Hatchet? I recall the case. Didn't she break into some safety-deposit boxes by chopping through the bank's outside wall?
Miss Maple. She made some such attempt.
Haversham (*ENTERS DOWN RIGHT*) But I didn't get away with it, and I done my time. I'd appreciate it, too, if you talked about me when I was in the room. It's only polite.
Louie. Murder and politeness seldom go together.
    (*THUNDER, the LIGHTS DIM UP and DOWN*)
Miss Maple. Will this cursed storm never end?
    (*Positions at this point should be roughly as follows:* **Charity** *and* **Miss Maple** *seated on the sofa.* **Chandler** *by the fireplace.* **Rita** *by the DOWNSTAGE end of sofa,* **Haversham** *DOWN RIGHT.* **Father White** *by the LEFT CENTER chair,* **Peter** *LEFT CENTER,* **Louie** *by the console.* **Laura** *by the doors*)
Charity. I can see where this is going to take a strong logical hand. (*She stands*) I think I can shed some light, too.
Peter. Please do.
    (**Father White** *sits,* **Peter** *moves a step LEFT.* **Charity** *moves CENTER*)

    (NOTE: From this point on as the various "deductions" and "suppositions" are considered, the **Cast** *acts and reacts in complete sincerity. It's the classic "suspects in the drawing room" finale*)
Charity. You're all agreed that the murderer used the tape recording to lay out his plan.
Peter. Carlyle's demise was proof.
Charity. Proof of nothing except that he was marked for death. Remember what I was accused of.
Father White. Murder.
Charity. Murder only in the figurative sense. What about it, Louie? What about the night in Shanghai?
Louie. Know nothing.
Charity. Remember the stakes. Survival.
    (*THUNDER*)
Father White. I'm thinking of something sinister.
Haversham. What?
Father White. There's one figurine left on the mantel.

Peter. If the killer is going to strike again, he'll have to do it before daylight.
Laura. I hope no one will say — "No one leave the room."

    (*All look at* **Louie**)

    (*As each* **Character** *"confesses" he has a moment's hesitation*)

Louie. Night in Shanghai does not refer to holiday in Orient. Rival writer was to use it for title of his new book. I used it first. He never forgave me.
Charity. My "murder" wasn't real; *Night in Shanghai* was nothing more than a book title. What about you, Mrs. Carlyle?
Laura. Me?
Charity. What does Tulip signify?
Laura. (*Fear and dismay*) Tulip was a dog, the sweetest little puppy you ever saw. I wanted to buy him, but the pet shop owner refused. He was adamant. He was going to sell him to a disagreeable and harsh Army major. I couldn't bear it, so Rick and I —
Charity. Dognappers.
Laura. We changed Tulip's name to Napoleon so no one would know. We were always afraid. How would it look on the society page?
Charity. What dark secret was yours, Chandler?
Laura. The recording said you couldn't escape your past. That you were guilty of a "foul crime."
Chandler. (*Moves behind sofa*) Do I have to?
Charity. (*Insistent*) Chandler!
Chandler. Well, uh, before I became a detective writer I had another job. I, uh —
Father White. You what?
Chandler. (*Swallows hard*) I was a literary critic.
Writers. Critic!
Laura. That is foul.
Peter. There's no sense asking me what happened on the playing fields of Eton. I haven't the slightest idea.

Charity. Don't you see. The recording is a joke. The "crimes" aren't crimes at all. Indiscretions, perhaps. Nothing more.

Miss Maple. As I was playing jokes here and there someone else was doing the same with the recording.
Charity. That's my guess. (*Sits on sofa*)
Chandler. I can buy it.
Laura. But who did it?
Chandler. We don't know if the tape recording and the murderer are one and the same. (*Moves DOWN CENTER*) Finding out the killer's identity is what's important. (*Moves to desk. All eyes following him*) What we have to decide is who had the motive and the opportunity to knock off Carlyle. (*Picks up pad and pencil*) The killer had to know the house.
Miss Maple. Could it have been the man in the dark glasses and scarf?
Chandler. Who?
Miss Maple. A moment before I was shot. He was in this room. Didn't I tell you? (*All shake their heads*) It must have slipped my mind. Do you think it was someone playing another little joke, enjoying the charade?
Chandler. Let me go on with my deducing.
Miss Maple. Please do, Chandler. I have faith in you.
Chandler. Remember those key words — "motive" — "opportunity."
> (*As **Chandler** starts to cross RIGHT, his foot somehow manages to get stuck in the wastebasket and he has trouble getting it out. All watch*)
Charity. Chandler, for goodness sake.
> (*TELEPHONE RINGS*)
Miss Maple. What's that?
Haversham. It's a telephone.
Miss Maple. There is no telephone on Turkey Island.
Rita. (*Moves STAGE LEFT*) It's coming from over here.
Laura. (*Points*) The desk.
Father White. There's no phone on the desk.
Chandler. (*Still busy with wastebasket, sits at desk*) Try the drawer.
> (**Rita** *opens one drawer, then another. PHONE CONTINUES to RING. She finds the phone, takes it out. All tense*)
Haversham. Answer it.
> (*Leery,* **Rita** *picks up the receiver*)

Rita. Ravenswood Manor.

Louie. Who is caller?

(**Rita** *frowns, listens a moment longer, puts down receiver, replaces it in the drawer*)

Miss Maple. What did they say?

Rita. I'd rather not repeat what I heard. The language was crude.

Charity. An obscene phone call at this hour?

Chandler. (*Ignoring the interruption*) Who had "motive" and who had "opportunity."

(*PHONE RINGS AGAIN. All tense*)

Chandler. Let me handle it. In the detective game you're either a firecracker or a fizzle. (*He stands, foot still in the wastebasket, opens drawer, takes out phone, lifts receiver*) This is Chandler Marlowe speaking, you pinhead. I have ways of tracing phone calls and when I find out who you are I'm going to rearrange your face. You're going to be breathing through your navel . . . (**Chandler**, *unlike* **Rita**, *has pulled the phone all the way out from the drawer so everyone can clearly see the cord is severed.* **Chandler** *continues on*) Is that so . . . you think you're man enough . . . you just remember my name, buster . . . Chandler Marlowe. (*He sees everyone glaring at him. He notices the severed cord, grins sheepishly, replaces the phone*)

Miss Maple. Mr. Marlowe, would you mind explaining?

Chandler. Uh, well, ha, ha. Part of the charade. You wanted us to keep it up, didn't you?

Charity. But the telephone rang.

Chandler. I've got a relay buzzer in my pocket. (*Sticks his hand in pocket, pretends to trigger some buzzer mechanism. PHONE RINGS*)

Haversham. Shall I answer it?

Miss Maple. Do shut up, you silly girl.

Rita. Better tell it all, Chandler.

Miss Maple. Rita, what do you have to do with this?

Rita. I'm Chandler's secretary.

Father White. You?

Rita. When Miss Maple advertised for a social secretary for one month, Chandler had me apply.

Chandler. I already had my invitation, so I thought it was a great opportunity for some laughs.
Miss Maple. Murder is no laughing matter.
Chandler. I kept needling Louie about the Headless Horseman until I had him thinking it was Rita who did the jockey in.
Louie. Interesting theory, but Louie Fan is not buying. Hat box undoubtedly contains blowdart gun that silenced Carlyle. (*He dashes to* **Rita,** *grabs hat box*)
Rita. Hey!
Louie. (*Rips off cover*) Behold! Murder weapon!
Father White. What's in there?
Louie. A head.
>   (**Miss Maple** *screams as does* **Haversham** *who, terrified, runs off DOWNSTAGE RIGHT*)
Peter. A head?
Louie. Head of cabbage.
Father White. Cabbage.
Rita. (*Takes back lid, replaces*) I called you a fool before and that's what you are. All part of the gag.
Louie. (*Moves UP STAGE*) Head of cabbage is food for thought.
Charity. Everything seems to be falling into place.
Laura. You forgot one thing, Miss Haze. Father White. He didn't confess to any "indiscretion." Not only that, he knows this house inside and out.
Father White. Why do you say that?
Laura. (*Points to bookcase*) Because I saw you coming out of that wall. There's a secret passageway back there.
Chandler. Secret passageway? Now we're getting somewhere.
Father White. Chandler is quite right. In detection we must always look for the unexpected. With the naked eye we cannot see the invisible snakes that exist in every glass of water.
Miss Maple. What's he going on about?
Father White. Invisible crocodiles that swim in every spoonful of soup.
Rita. Soup?
Father White. Or the invisible dolphins that roam and play in every droplet of milk.

Peter. What are you getting at?

Chandler. That's the sort of stuff he puts in his books. Nobody can understand it.

Father White. I merely wish to point out that we must employ a microscope of the mind when we "investigate."

(The others look uneasily from one to another. They haven't understood a word)

Chandler. If you say so.

Father White. *(Resigned)* I suppose there's no point in continuing the deception. *(All tense)* Truth of the matter is — I'm not Father White.

Miss Maple. Impossible.

Rita. Who are you?

Father White. A strolling minstrel, you might say. I'm an actor.

Miss Maple. I never invite actors.

Father White. They're doing a new radio series on Father White, so I persuaded the real invitee to allow me to take his place. To test my impersonation. To get "inside" the mind of Father White. To act and react as he would —

Miss Maple. That's quite enough of that drivel. Invisible crocodiles, indeed.

Laura. But the secret passageway?

Rita. It's not a secret passageway. The original owner had a flair for eccentric architecture. It leads up from the wine cellar.

Miss Maple. Oh, is that where the other door is.

Peter. Didn't you know?

Miss Maple. Ravenswood Manor isn't my home. I merely rented it for a few weeks for the purpose of this weekend house party.

(SOUND of HELICOPTER)

Chandler. Listen!

Rita. The helicopter.

Miss Maple. Maybe this time it is the police.

(All rush to doors)

Laura. Can you see it?

Louie. Too dark.

Miss Maple. Is it at the dock or over the house?

Chandler. I think it's on the north side of the island.

Charity. We could signal with a flare.

Chandler. Through the kitchen. Out that way.
(*All rush DOWNSTAGE RIGHT. During this distraction,* **Charity** *slips out the doors.* **Rita** *remains by the desk.* **Chandler** *is still fighting the wastebasket*)
Father White. Signalling the helicopter may be our last chance.
Miss Maple. We must get its attention.
(*SOUND of HELICOPTER FADES. Bookcase slowly swings open*)
Rita. *Wait! Look!*
(*Others stop and turn at* **Rita's** *words. All stare at bookcase. A moment passes and the INDIVIDUAL MISS MAPLE saw previously, still dressed in hat, glasses, gloves, long coat, ENTERS*)
Miss Maple. It's him. The man I was telling you about!
(*There is a moment of dramatic suspense as the man in the passageway takes off the hat, the scarf, the glasses*)
Father White. Good Lord — *Rick Carlyle!*
Miss Maple. It's not possible. You're dead.
Chandler. Never saw anyone deader.
Rick. (*Moves STAGE CENTER*) I, too, thought of a little joke that would be amusing. Instead of one Rick Carlyle there would be two.
Louie. Two?
Laura. Rick's twin brother. He's the one down in the wine cellar.
Rick. I was going to confuse everyone, be in two places at the same time. Only someone got to me first and finished me off.
Chandler. You mean your brother, don't you?
Rick. That's right. Only the murderer didn't know he had made a mistake. so I decided to stay out of sight and learn what I could.
Chandler. (*Still struggling with the wastebasket*) What did you learn?
Rick. Nothing.
Peter. (*His voice and manner are slightly different*) I'll take it from here.
Louie. (*Points*) You — you are the murderer.
Peter. How can anyone be so consistently wrong?

Miss Maple. You'll take what from here?

Peter. (*Moves CENTER*) The investigation. I saw Carlyle talking with his brother in town. Carlyle's twin was a con-artist. If he was coming here, he had plans to rob. Flimsey owes me a favor or two, so he was no problem.

Rick. My brother was no good, that's true. He did seem to agree rather quickly. I should have suspected.

Peter. The pickings would be good. Some jewels, some wallets. Who knows what else?

Charity. If you're not Peter Flimsey, who are you?

        (*He takes out an I.D. wallet, displays badge*)

Peter. Pharaoh Link.

Chandler. Crack investigator on the 'Frisco force.

Peter. (*Corrects*) That's *San Francisco*. Can't you get your foot out of that wastebasket?

Chandler. I'm trying.

        (**Haversham** *ENTERS DOWN RIGHT.* **Chand-**
        ler *pulls out his foot.* **Peter** *moves LEFT*)

Miss Maple. (*Sits on sofa*) Everything has been explained satisfactorily.

        (**Haversham** *edges up to fireplace*)

Rita. Not quite.

Miss Maple. It was all a charming and delightful exercise in now-you-see it, now-you-don't.

        (**Haversham** *stands UP CENTER*)

Rita. Who killed the man in the wine cellar!!!

        (**Haversham** *speaks out, her voice strong, power-*
        ful, threatening)

Haversham. Let me answer that! (*Fast, she pulls off*
her glasses, fluffs out her hair and strips off the too-
large dress to reveal a shapely figure dressed in the
latest chic fashion)

Peter. Who are you, Miss?

Rick. *Mabel!*

Laura. Mabel? Oh, Rick. (**Laura** *goes into* **Rick's**
arms)

Louie. (*Points at* **Haversham**) You — you are the murderer.

Charity. If you say that one more time, I'll murder *you*.

        (**Mabel** *lifts the hem of her short skirt. There's*
        a small pistol secure in the top of her hose. She
        pulls it out, aims)

Mabel. I mean business. (*To* **Rick**) I killed the wrong man, but I won't make that mistake a second time. No one leave this room.

Miss Maple. Where is the real Haversham?

Mabel. Probably in Canada by now. I gave her two hundred dollars to take her place.

Miss Maple. I won't be able to give a very good report to the parole people.

Peter. I wouldn't shoot.

Mabel. He made a fool of me. No one walks out on Mabel Dupre. I've killed one man already, what does another one matter?

Laura. Rick, she's going to shoot!
  (*General pandemonium as* **Charity** *leaps in from UP CENTER, gives the firing wrist a karate chop, the GUN FIRES into the carpet.* **Charity** *jumps behind* **Mabel** *and gets her in a backarm lock*)

Chandler. What a woman!

Miss Maple. You're a wonder.

Peter. The police helicopter is flying around to see if I need assistance. It's going to have an unexpected passenger. I'm taking you in.
  (*He moves to* **Mabel,** *puts on a pair of cuffs*)

Miss Maple. Look, it's dawn.
  (*All look to the doors. If possible, a BRIGHT LIGHTING EFFECT is brought in from outside to simulate.the blazing dawn*)

Father White. And the storm has passed. That means the boat from the mainland will be here soon.

Peter. (*Pushing her out*) Come along, Mabel. You've got a date with the jury.

Mabel. (*Head high*) I won't have anything to worry about. Not if there are twelve men on that jury.
  (**Peter** *and* **Mabel** *EXIT*)

Laura. I don't want to stay in this place another minute.

Father White. Let's get our luggage and let's get out of here.
  (**Chandler, Father White, Louie, Rick** *and* **Laura** *move UP CENTER*)

Charity. I didn't bring any luggage. Maybe I can hitch a ride with Pharaoh Link. He's my kind of man. (**Charity** *EXITS LEFT*)

Chandler. What about me? How do you like that? I should know better than to trust a dame. (*He shakes his head like the cynical cuss he is, EXITS UP CENTER after the others*)
Miss Maple. Rita, see if you can get something on the radio besides static.
      (**Rita** *moves to console, snaps it on*)
Miss Maple. I do hope they'll send someone for the gentleman in the wine cellar.
Rita. I'm sure they will.
Miss Maple. What a night, what a night.
Radio. We interrupt this program of light chamber music to bring you a special bulletin. A dangerous murderer has escaped from the Marin County Institute for the Criminally Insane. Known only as "The Killer of Forty Faces," etc.
Miss Maple. Turn it off, Rita. (**Rita** *snaps it off.* **Miss Maple** *addresses audience directly*) We don't want to go through that again.

CURTAIN

END OF PLAY

PRODUCTION NOTES

Stage Properties

Fireplace with mantel, three figurines, portrait, console, bookcase with books (secret passageway), desk with paper and pencil, wastebasket, telephone (in drawer). ADDITIONAL STAGE DRESSING (rugs, lamps, small tables, chairs, etc.) — as desired.

Hand and Personal Properties

ACT ONE: Hat box (**Rita**), eyeglasses (**Miss Maple**), umbrella (**Father White**), fan (**Louie**), toy dog (**Rick**), gun (**Chandler**), tray with plate of biscuits and glasses of sherry (**Haversham**); ACT TWO: flashlight (**Father

White), magnifying glass (**Peter**), afghan (**Rita**); ACT
THREE: newspaper clipping (**Louie**), I.D. wallet with
badge (**Peter**), gun (**Haversham**), handcuffs (**Peter**).

Sound Effects

Motorboat, gunshots, helicopter, voice making accusations, storm effects, telephone. All required sound effects available through Baker's. Consult our catalogue.
(Motor Boat, No. 1025; Helicopter, No. 1016.)

Costumes

Mentioned here are only those costumes somehow necessary to plot: large maid's dress, eyeglasses (**Haversham**), raincoat, hat (**Chandler**), raincoat and hat
(**Louie**), goggles, helmet, raincoat (**Charity**).

Some nice visual touches can be made in costuming, if
desired. For example, **Rick** and **Laura** might arrive
in evening clothes, **Louie** could wear a floor-length
Oriental robe, **Charity** might arrive in a jumpsuit, etc.

In the program be sure to list the roles of **Mabe Dupre**
and **Pharaoh Link**. This way the audience assumes
two "new" characters are always about to appear and
shed some light on the mystery. The **Radio Voice** must
come across *LOUD* and *CLEAR*. Try and make the
"unveiling" of **Haversham/Mabel Dupre** as effective
as possible. If the actress could use a wig — great. And
it helps if her "Mabel" costume under the maid's outfit
is eye-catching. In the third act be careful not to rush
the dialog because there's much that the audience has
to digest and speed will only cut down on the laughs
and minimize the overall effect. Pauses and reactions
are most important here. Remember that characters are
always entering and exiting through the double or French
doors, so make certain they are closed after a character
has entered or left. A door that stands open on stage,
especially in a thriller script, always diverts attention.
Mabel's pistol shot can come from off stage, actress
doesn't have to actually fire the prop.

SAMUEL FRENCH STAFF

Nate Collins
President

Ken Dingledine
Director of Operations,
Vice President

Bruce Lazarus
Executive Director,
General Counsel

Rita Maté
Director of Finance

ACCOUNTING
Lori Thimsen | Director of Licensing Compliance
Nehal Kumar | Senior Accounting Associate
Helena Mezzina | Royalty Administration
Glenn Halcomb | Royalty Administration
Jessica Zheng | Accounts Receivable
Andy Lian | Accounts Payable
Charlie Sou | Accounting Associate
Joann Mannello | Orders Administrator

CUSTOMER SERVICE AND LICENSING
Brad Lohrenz | Director of Licensing Development
Laura Lindson | Licensing Services Manager
Kim Rogers | Theatrical Specialist
Matthew Akers | Theatrical Specialist
Ashley Byrne | Theatrical Specialist
Jennifer Carter | Theatrical Specialist
Annette Storckman | Theatrical Specialist
Dyan Flores | Theatrical Specialist
Sarah Weber | Theatrical Specialist
Nicholas Dawson | Theatrical Specialist
Andrew Clarke| Theatrical Specialist
David Kimple | Theatrical Specialist

EDITORIAL
Amy Rose Marsh | Literary Manager
Ben Coleman | Editorial Associate
Caitlin Bartow | Assistant to the Executive Director

MARKETING
Abbie Van Nostrand | Director of Corporate
    Communications
Ryan Pointer | Marketing Manager
Courtney Kochuba | Marketing Associate

PUBLICATIONS AND PRODUCT DEVELOPMENT
Joe Ferreira | Product Development Manager
David Geer | Publications Manager
Charlyn Brea | Publications Associate
Tyler Mullen | Publications Associate
Derek P. Hassler | Musical Products Coordinator
Zachary Orts | Musical Materials Coordinator

OPERATIONS
Casey McLain | Operations Supervisor
Elizabeth Minski | Office Coordinator, Reception
Coryn Carson | Office Coordinator, Reception

SAMUEL FRENCH BOOKSHOP (LOS ANGELES)
Joyce Mehess | Bookstore Manager
Cory DeLair | Bookstore Buyer
Jennifer Palumbo | Bookstore Order Dept. Manager
Sonya Wallace | Bookstore Associate
Tim Coultas | Bookstore Associate
Alfred Contreras | Shipping & Receiving

LONDON OFFICE
Felicity Barks | Rights & Contracts Associate
Steve Blacker | Bookshop Associate
David Bray | Customer Services Associate
Zena Choi | Professional Licensing Associate
Robert Cooke | Assistant Buyer
Stephanie Dawson | Amateur Licensing Associate
Simon Ellison | Retail Sales Manager
Jason Felix | Royalty Administration
Susan Griffiths | Amateur Licensing Associate
Robert Hamilton | Amateur Licensing Associate
Lucy Hume | Publications Manager
Nasir Khan | Management Accountant
Simon Magniti | Royalty Administration
Louise Mappley | Amateur Licensing Associate
James Nicolau | Despatch Associate
Martin Phillips | Librarian
Zubayed Rahman | Despatch Associate
Steve Sanderson | Royalty Administration Supervisor
Douglas Schatz | Acting Executive Director
Roger Sheppard | I.T. Manager
Panos Panayi | Company Accountant
Peter Smith | Amateur Licensing Associate
Garry Spratley | Customer Service Manager
David Webster | UK Operations Director